This Book
Belongs To:

_____

_____

First published 2018 © Twinkl Ltd of Wards Exchange, 197 Ecclesall Road, Sheffield S11 8HW

ISBN: 978-1-914331-29-9

We're passionate about giving our children a sustainable future, which is why this book is made from Forest Stewardship Council® certified paper. Learn how our Twinkl Green policy gives the planet a helping hand at www.twinkl.com/twinkl-green.

Printed in the United Kingdom.

10 9 8 7 6 5 4 3 2 1

A catalogue record for this book is available from the British Library.

Twinkl is a registered trademark of Twinkl Ltd.

A TWINKL ORIGINAL

CODE-CRACKING
FOR BEGINNERS

Twinkl Educational Publishing

CONTENTS

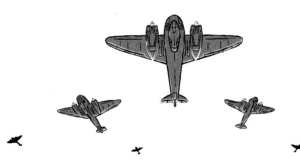

Chapter One
Sirens and Strays

Death was coming. It would fall from the skies like a hail of deadly meteors – not dropped by some malevolent force from outer space, but spawned in the iron bellies of Hitler's deadly Luftwaffe bombers.

Sirens wailed their nightly warning, conducting a drumbeat of frightened feet across the pavements of London's East End. Streams of panicked citizens spewed through the narrow streets; children screamed their resistance as mothers and fathers hauled them through jostling crowds. Wardens barked orders and pointed instructions at the hordes, but few people paid any attention. They were too fearful

1

of the fire and fury that was roaring over the English Channel towards them. Terror had already turned happy, young faces into ugly balls of fear, and the eyes of thousands were turned constantly upwards, pulled wide and white by dread.

Eleven-year-old Samuel Hunt watched all of this from beside the mouth of Bethnal Green tube station. He had long since grown used to the sirens and fright that gripped his city most evenings. For him, the piercing howl was oddly reassuring – a sign that life and London were still functioning. What he feared much more was the silence that came afterwards. That was where the Grim Reaper's work could usually be found.

"Better head down the steps, Sammy," a familiar voice urged. The heavy-set butcher's wife herded her two toddlers past him. "Adolf's bombs can't reach you down on the tube."

Sam smiled a thank-you. "I'll be down in a minute, Missus Griffiths – just as soon as Lily gets here."

"Don't let that cousin of yours be the death of you, Samuel Hunt," Mrs Griffiths warned as the crowd swept her and her children down into the underground station. "You've got to look after yourself in times like these."

Sam wasn't listening. He was too preoccupied with scanning the faces that were pouring towards him. He searched anxiously for the ones that belonged to his family.

"Sammy! Sammy!"

He saw the waving arms before he pinpointed their owner. A wave of relief swept goosebumps down his arms as his blue eyes locked onto a pair that were almost identical to his own. The beacon of red hair that bobbed in the sea of hats and scarves could only belong to one person.

"Mum! Over here!" Sam waved back, knowing that his own thatch of red hair would guide his mother straight to him.

He felt the squeeze of pure love as his mother enveloped him in a hug. She planted a warm kiss on his cheek, then landed a sharp slap across the back of his head.

"How many times have I told you not to wait?" Joan Hunt growled at her son. "The Germans won't wait until you're safe before they drop those blasted bombs."

"Dad told me that I'm the man of the house while he's away," Sam reminded his mother. "I'm just doing what he would do."

"Well, he would want you to be safe," Joan snapped. "You're only eleven, Sammy. That's far too young to be a hero."

Sam peered over his mother's shoulder. Although he'd only just turned eleven, he was already several inches taller than her. "Where are Aunt

Peg and Lily?"

"Where we should both be, if they've got any sense," Joan told her son. "They're probably keeping us a space clear beside the heating vents." She shivered and pulled the collar of her woollen coat up around her ears. It wasn't yet autumn but there was an early chill to the late August evening.

"But I haven't seen them yet," Sam said, searching the crowd for a set of familiar auburn curls, "and I've been here since the sirens started."

It was unusual for his mother not to be accompanied by her sister and young niece. The two families lived on neighbouring streets and usually did everything together. His cousin Lily spent so much time at Sam's house that their relationship felt more like that of a brother and sister.

Sam watched a veil of worry slip across his mother's freckled face. "The house was empty when I passed," she told him. "I thought they'd be here."

"Get down those steps," an angry voice barked behind them.

Sam didn't need to look over his shoulder to know that it belonged to a warden called Jack. The booming voice and bullying tone were almost as familiar as the air raid sirens.

A heavy hand shoved against Sam's shoulder, spinning him towards the station's stairwell.

"You're blocking the entrance," the warden growled. "That's how people get killed."

Sam steered his mother towards a huddle of families heading to the safety of the stairs. When she was locked between two waddling grandmothers, he whispered, "I'll meet you by the cigarette machine."

"What? No!" His mother twisted and threw a hand out towards him, but Sam moved too quickly. Her straining fingertips lightly grazed his shoulder as he dodged back towards the street. "Samm-eeeee!"

"It'll only take a minute," he assured her,

watching the crowd carry his mother towards the underground sanctuary. Then, he added under his breath, "Dad would want me to check."

*

The streets of Bethnal Green were deserted. Even the wind seemed to have been chased away by the sirens. Everywhere looked frozen in time and, as he navigated his way across the paved streets, Sam felt like an intruder.

He was surprised to see a trio of bewildered dogs cross his path. The fugitive terriers trotted round a corner and paused to stare at him, their little, dark eyes shining like buttons. Sam hoped that a friendly smile would put them at ease – beneath their coats of matted fur, they looked half starved and he felt sorry for them. Once beloved family pets, the dogs no longer had owners or homes and ran a daily gauntlet of danger. They now survived on what scraps of food they could scavenge and the goodwill of strangers, even though it was an offence to feed them.

Despite all this, Sam knew that these dogs were

the lucky ones – they were still alive. Since Winston Churchill's government had banned the ownership of pets, hundreds of thousands had simply vanished from the country's streets. Sam still remembered shedding a tear when he'd read the Home Office pamphlet telling owners what to do with their 'non-essential animals'.

"Food is rationed, now, and the animals would only panic during the air raids," his mother had explained. "There's no other way, Sam... blame Hitler, not Mister Churchill."

Sam had been glad that they hadn't owned a dog or a cat, but that didn't stop him from now wanting to reach out and comfort the mangy strays. Before he had a chance, the largest of the three gave a yelp and the trio bolted for the nearest alley – probably pursuing the scent of a tasty rat or mouse.

"Good luck," Sam whispered after them as he broke into a trot himself, heading in the opposite direction.

The haze of twilight was beginning to fall across the borough like a shawl. The street lights no longer functioned and London would fall into total darkness as soon as the sun dipped below the horizon. If Sam didn't reach the underground before night fell, he'd have to take his chances against the Luftwaffe's merciless cargo.

As his legs carried him onto the narrow street that he called home, a sound as familiar as that of his own breathing told him that he wasn't the only resident not yet taking shelter in the underground.

"Lily!" His aunt Peg's voice was shrill with

panic. "Where are you, Lily? LILY!"

Sam found his mother's sister roaming the next street, frantically pounding on locked and silent doors. Tears of worry and fear had already made her freckled cheeks shiny.

"Has anyone seen my daughter?" Peg yelled desperately as she pressed her face against the glass of a darkened window. "Lily, are you in there?"

"These houses are empty." Sam's voice made his aunt gasp with shock. "Everyone is on the tracks."

His mother's younger sister rushed towards him, grabbing Sam's shoulders and hugging him. Spirals of red hair tickled his cheeks. He breathed in her familiar scent; she wore the same cheap perfume as his mother.

Peg wiped the tears from her eyes and fixed her nephew with what was supposed to be a glare. "What are you doing here, Samuel Hunt? Where's your mother?"

"She sent me to get you," he lied. "Lily, too."

Hope briefly softened his aunt's glare. "So, you know where she is?"

Without replying, Sam took his aunt's hand and guided her along the pavement. Black shadows were chasing away the last strands of daylight, now, but even in the thickening gloom, Sam navigated their route with ease. He'd always boasted that he could find his secret hiding place blindfolded – this was his chance to prove it.

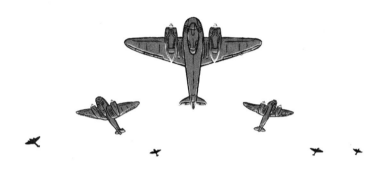

Chapter Two
Hoot like an Owl

The narrow residential streets of Bethnal Green were surrounded by old mills and warehouses, many now derelict or partly destroyed. These were dangerous places with crumbling walls and rotting beams, and the borough's children were forbidden to play there. Sam and his friends rarely listened.

"What are we doing here?" Aunt Peg whispered as Sam led them both through the twisted metal gates of a once-bustling weaving mill. "These places are dangerous."

"Where do you think us kids go when you tell us to clear out of the house?" Sam said. "It's not like we've got fields and woods to explore like kids in the country – this is London."

"There are lots of safer places to go," Aunt Peg insisted. "I'm surprised that not one of you has been killed in this place. And what's that smell? It's disgusting!"

Like most of the other children, Sam had grown accustomed to the pungent cocktail of rot and decay. He thought it best not to mention that rats and other stray animals regularly left smelly calling cards.

"Why would my Lily come here instead of the underground station?" Aunt Peg continued, her brow creased and her eyes narrowed. She brushed her hand against the crumbling brickwork. "It seems like a strong wind could flatten this place, never mind one of Jerry's doodlebugs."

The last glow of daylight was too weak to reach into the derelict mill and Sam's footsteps were slow and careful. He was seeing with his fingertips, now, guided by familiar textures and creaks from the floor. As though it had been expecting him, a cool gust of stale air reached them up a steep flight of stone steps, drawing their journey to a halt.

"Are we here?" Aunt Peg asked. A small hand rested softly on her nephew's shoulder and her tight breathing told Sam that she was afraid.

Outside, the growing hum of Luftwaffe engines had replaced the screeching sirens. It sounded like a swarm of a million bees was heading straight for them. Aunt Peg's fingers tightened around Sam's shoulder in an anxious grip.

"We're close," Sam told her. "She's probably at the bottom of those steps."

"Probably? You mean we might have come through this death trap for nothing?"

Sam ignored the question, deflecting it with one of his own. "Can you hoot like an owl?"

"What?"

"One of us needs to make a sound like an owl," Sam explained. "It's our secret signal."

"Secret bloomin' signal?" his aunt spluttered. "We aren't playing stupid spy games."

"She won't let us in if one of us doesn't hoot," he assured her. "I've never been very good at it. Lily says I sound more like a constipated seagull."

"I don't like the sound of this," Aunt Peg admitted. "What do you mean, she won't let us in? Let us in *where*?"

Sam sighed. Aunt Peg asked more questions than his mother; he had always thought that she would make a great army interrogator.

"Listen. It's pointless going down into the basement if she isn't there, but we won't know that unless one of us hoots."

"If this is some kind of wind-up, I'll give your ears a box," warned his aunt as she prepared to hoot. "And don't you dare laugh at me, Samuel Hunt!"

It was difficult not to snigger, at least. Aunt Peg's owl impression was worse than his and a sound resembling the squeal of a startled bat sent a small flock of pigeons fleeing from the rafters above. Peg froze, listening intently with wide eyes. As she drew a second breath, preparing to frighten more of the local wildlife, a much clearer sound floated up from the basement beneath them.

"Was that a real owl?" Aunt Peg asked, confused.

Grabbing his aunt's hand, Sam gingerly began to descend the damp, stone steps. There were thirteen in total; he'd counted them many times. Most were covered in a thin film of slippery, green moss.

Despite a couple of slips, the two climbers reached the final step unscathed. Their feet landed on solid ground, and a darkness that only coal miners could comprehend surrounded them completely.

"This way," Sam urged as he skimmed the damp wall with his fingertips. The lip of a worn, wooden shelf told him that their destination was less than a yard away. This was confirmed when his palm struck cold brickwork, sending a sharp slap rolling through the darkness. Concern wrapped his aunt's fingers tightly around his own.

"Don't worry," he reassured her. "We're here."

"Where's *here*?" Aunt Peg asked. "I can't see a thing."

Before Sam had a chance to reply, the unnatural clang of metal scraping on metal rang out. This was followed by the rusty squeak of reluctant hinges as a door opened wide in front of them. Light from the flame of an orange lamp poured into the basement, momentarily blinding them both.

"Sam? Is that you?" enquired a young girl's voice.

Lily Taylor's ten-year-old face peered out into the darkness as she swung her lantern left and then right. The orange glow made her red hair shine brighter than a bonfire's flame and her green eyes sparkled like emeralds. Shock stretched them wide when her gaze found the faces of the two visitors. "Mum? What are you doing here?"

Aunt Peg pushed past Sam, rushing to grasp her daughter's arm. It was far from a friendly caress. "I should be asking you the same thing! Why aren't you at the underground station like everyone else?"

Lily squirmed to escape her mother's grip. "I don't like it in the tunnels, Mum. There are too many people and it smells."

"What? And you think this stinking place is better?" Her mother snatched Lily's lantern and waved it in front of herself. Her eyes widened in her pale, tear-streaked face as the light revealed that her daughter was leaning through the storage hatch of a large, industrial coal bunker.

"It's safer down here, Mum, honest!" Lily insisted. "If a bomb falls, the building will take the hit."

Sam slapped the bunker's red brickwork. Rows of smooth, kiln-fired bricks made the bunker seem impregnable. "She's right."

Aunt Peg shook her head. "If you two think I'm spending the night locked inside that thing, you've got another –"

The rest of her sentence lodged in her throat as, somewhere above them, the first rumbles of falling bombs echoed across the country's capital city like thunderclaps. The ground trembled around them.

"We'll never make it to the station," Sam told his aunt, "and there's plenty of room inside here."

As the rumbles grew louder and nearer, his aunt gave the two young cousins a withering glare before clambering through the bunker's hatch. She coughed as she breathed in coal dust. "If we get out of this thing alive, you two are going to be in serious trouble."

Chapter Three
Gas Masks and Backpacks

"Is this our punishment?" Lily whispered to her cousin as herds of sobbing children streamed past them. "Is that why we're being sent away?"

It had been less than a week since they had sheltered in the old mill's coal bunker and, despite surviving several nights of Luftwaffe bombing raids since, they now faced what felt like a much worse threat: evacuation.

Sam snaked a comforting arm around his younger cousin. "Mum says it's for our own protection. London's just getting too dangerous."

They both coughed as a thick billow of acrid steam spewed from the locomotive in front of them, engulfing them entirely. Two aching faces seemed to float down through the cloud towards them.

"It won't be for long," Sam's mother promised. "The war will be over soon and then everything will be back to normal."

The tears that fell like tiny jewels from the corners of his mother's eyes told Sam that she didn't believe those words.

Aunt Peg dabbed her own eyes with a damp handkerchief before planting a kiss on her daughter's cheek. "There are loving families waiting up north to take good care of you," she sniffed. "It'll be like having a second mother – and there will be woodlands and meadows to play in, not those stinking derelict buildings."

"But I like those stinking buildings," Lily blubbed. "They're *our* stinking buildings. I don't want to go up north. You didn't send us away last time."

Sam remembered the last time. It had been two years earlier, straight after war had been declared. Half of his classmates had vanished overnight, evacuated to all corners of the country. Some had even found themselves in Scotland.

Several had come back, weeks later, but most had remained missing from the school register. Their empty school desks and chairs became a daily reminder of their absence. Now, it seemed that Sam and Lily would be added to that list.

All around them, hundreds of mothers and children were having nearly identical conversations. The distressed howls and cries of families being separated were almost loud enough to drown out the chuffs and wheezes from the waiting trains. Carriages already bustled with reluctant children. Most were hanging out of the windows, begging to be taken home.

"Think of it as being like one big adventure," Aunt Peg suggested, "or an extended holiday – how exciting is that?"

As Lily argued that she didn't want to go on holiday, especially one that didn't include her mother, Joan Hunt waved a couple of large, cardboard labels towards the two children.

"You're actually very lucky," she said as she began to tie the first label to the buckle of Sam's brown cotton rucksack.

She had packed her son's bag the night before. They'd both been aghast at the few items of clothing that they were allowed to pack, but the government's instructions had been very clear: the evacuees were to travel light.

Still, just two vests and two pairs of underpants, a single pair of trousers and only one jersey or pullover hardly seemed enough for a weekend away, let alone weeks or perhaps even months in a strange town. Sam had squeezed a couple more items in, stuffing extra pants and socks deep into the toes of his boots, and his mum had rolled two additional shirts tightly into the pockets of his overcoat. But that was the only extra clothing that they had dared to stash, just in case the bag was checked at the station.

"How is Lily supposed to survive with just one extra pair of knickers?" Aunt Peg had complained as they had approached King's Cross station. "I've told her to wear three pairs beneath her skirt but even that's not enough. And I don't care what they say about only packing one blouse – I've hidden two more in her rolled-up cardigan."

The rucksack's large side pockets bulged with sandwiches made from the last of their hoarded rations. Nestled between his two pairs of underpants, half hidden by a facecloth that was folded around Sam's toothbrush, comb and soap, was half a bar of chocolate. It would make for a much tastier treat than the nuts, raisins and barley sugar that they were allowed to take with them.

Aunt Peg seemed to gasp in genuine delight as she read from the second label. "Scarborough! It says you're both going to Scarborough." She looked across at her sister. "We've always wanted to go there, haven't we, Joan?"

Sam's mother nodded. Her face showed none of her sister's happiness. "Apparently, it's a beautiful place, and people from Yorkshire are so friendly. You'll be well looked after."

Sam screwed his face up tight. "Yorkshire? Isn't it meant to be freezing cold up there?"

"It's not the North Pole, Samuel Hunt," Aunt Peg reminded him. "I'm sure that the sun shines just as brightly in Yorkshire as it does in London."

"So, why can't you come with us, Mum?" Lily wept. She'd barely stopped snivelling since they had arrived at King's Cross station.

Aunt Peg shook her head. "Your Aunt Joan and I have both got important jobs. Those navy uniforms won't sew themselves, Lily. We've all got to pitch in if we're going to win this war."

"Well, you won't defeat Jerry by standing on this platform," a red-faced man told them loudly. He stared down at a sheet of paper pinned to a board. The man leaned back against a large metal strut, apparently glad of the break. "Who do we have here?"

"Samuel Hunt and Lily Taylor," Sam's mother said.

The man scanned the sheet of paper. It was filled with several columns of names and destinations. His finger ran up and down the columns like a rollercoaster carriage until it stopped abruptly.

"Here you are: Samuel and Lily. You're both allocated seats on the eleven-forty train to York."

He turned his head and craned backwards to catch sight of the station's huge clock. When he saw the time, his eyebrows sprang to attention. His voice was suddenly thick with worry. "It leaves in seven minutes. You'll be lucky to get a seat together – standing room only all the way."

As the man turned to leave, Sam's mum grasped

his wrist. "They're cousins. More like brother and sister." The man offered a weary shrug.

Aunt Peg gripped his other arm, holding him hostage. "We don't want them to be separated. They must stay together."

"I just deal with departures, sweetheart..." he told her. Perhaps it was the two anxious scowls that prompted him to continue. "...but I'm sure the authorities in Yorkshire will do all they can. The host families receive eight shillings a week and extra rations for each child. I reckon they'll be fighting each other to look after two lovely children like yours."

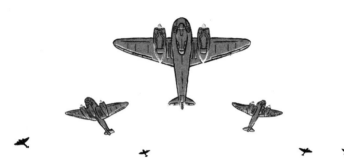

Chapter Four
It's Called Yorkshire

The train journey from London to York felt like it would never end. After exploring the long snake of carriages several times, the two cousins eventually squeezed into what might have been the last two available seats. Their position outside one of the train's few toilet cubicles perhaps explained why they had remained unclaimed.

At first, the carriages bustled with noise and movement. Many children sobbed loudly or tried to comfort friends. Yet there were just as many who seemed excited to be leaving London. These laughed cheerfully or leaned out of their windows to wave at people in the towns and villages which flew past. One group of boys even sang several songs, encouraging the rest of their carriage to beat an accompanying rhythm on their gas mask boxes.

After that first noisy hour, though, the train grew mostly silent. The adult wardens and stewards encouraged this with shouts of "Pipe down!" and "Keep it shut!" whenever chit-chat or laughter threatened to erupt. Sam was thankful for the peace; Lily had already cried herself into a fitful sleep.

The gentle rocking of the train on its tracks was threatening to turn Sam's own eyelids to lead when a voice pulled him from the brink of slumber.

"You know much about this Scarborough place?"

Sam rubbed his eyes open and blinked the world into focus. He recognised the boy peering down at him. Tom Mahoney was a year younger than him and quite a lot smaller.

"Not really," Sam told him. "Rich folk used to go there on their holidays, I think. Not sure many people do that, now."

"My grandma says they've got a whopping great fishing fleet up there – hundreds of trawlers, by all accounts." Tom's blue eyes sparkled with enthusiasm. He ran a small hand through a twist of blonde hair which looked as though it hadn't seen a comb for days. "I hope one of the fishermen's wives takes me in. I'd love to go out to sea."

Sam nodded, though he couldn't think of anything worse. He remembered his dad taking them out onto the Serpentine Lake in a rowing boat before he'd been called up. The small waves caused by other rowers had made him feel ill – the thought of going out onto the rough North Sea was enough to chill his blood.

"What kind of family are you hoping for?" Tom asked.

Sam shook his head. "Dunno, Tom. I haven't really thought about it. Someone kind, I reckon. With a house big enough to take our Lily, too."

Tom glanced across at Sam's sleeping cousin.

Doubt twitched his nose. "You'll be lucky, Sam. She's not your sister. The bloke on the platform told our mum that the priority is for siblings. Shame you haven't got the same surname, eh?"

"Well, there'll be trouble if they try separating us," Sam warned. "I'm going nowhere without Lil."

*

The platform at York station was heaving and, as the weary children stumbled out of the carriages, space soon became scarce. They all juggled various bags and boxes of different sizes – some even clutched parcels wrapped in brown paper and string – and it wasn't long before they were all squashed side by side like pencils in a box.

Sam and Lily had been the first off the train and were pressed into an alcove next to the station's ticket booth, which was plastered with posters and pamphlets bearing the familiar four words: **CARELESS TALK COSTS LIVES**. These particular images showed pairs of passengers seated on buses and trains, gossiping while narrow-eyed military leaders listened in from the seats behind.

These reminders did nothing to ease the children's nerves. Elbows clashed as the older boys jostled for room. Cross words and raised voices made it obvious that fights and scuffles weren't far away. Fortunately, this hadn't gone unnoticed and the shrill bellow of a tall, thick-limbed woman quickly brought some order.

"QUI-ET!"

The entire platform quickly fell silent.

"That's quite enough of your racket, thank you very much," she told them. Her tone was as firm and strong as the strides that she took along the platform. "My name is Missus Scales."

She was wrapped in a brown woollen coat, held tight around her waist by a leather belt. Both looked as though they had once belonged to her husband – in fact, the only nod to feminine fashion was a red headscarf, which seemed to struggle to contain a straining nest of black and grey hair.

"You're in Yorkshire, now, boys and girls." The thick soles of her boots thumped the platform like blocks of wood as she prowled before the group. "We do stuff differently up 'ere. We do things *properly*. An' we won't stand for no nonsense. D'you understand?"

A murmur of uncertainty rustled from one child to the next as they exchanged whispers and shrugs. Mrs Scales narrowed her eyes as strong arms folded across her chest.

"I said, d'you understand?" The last word was spat loud enough to make several girls whimper.

"Good. Right, let's get this sorted, then," the woman continued. Her weather-reddened cheeks wobbled as she spoke. "The easier you lot make this, the quicker you'll be off to your new homes an' families, an' the sooner I can get back to doin' proper work on me farm."

Mrs Scales stopped to glance down at the row of children in front of her. Her eyes settled on Tom Mahoney. "By 'eck, lad, I bet tha's never seen t' back end of a cow, am I right?"

"Uh... I..." Tom's lips quivered as he struggled to form words. "I stroked a horse, once."

Mrs Scales' face cracked into a cruel grin and she unleashed a bellowing laugh. Tom looked at his feet; blotches of pink appeared on his pale cheeks. "Well, lad, you'd better get used to some 'ard work up 'ere. This isn't a holiday!"

Lily nudged her cousin lightly in the ribs as she whispered, "What kind of English is she speaking, Sam?"

Without taking his eyes off Mrs Scales, Sam replied, "I think it's called Yorkshire."

The woman was joined by a team of equally no-nonsense helpers and soon, the large flock of confused evacuees was being herded into smaller, more manageable groups. The booming voice of Mrs Scales controlled everything, managing operations like a conductor directing an orchestra.

"Bridlington, go to t' left. Malton and Pickering to t' right," she instructed as her assistants checked the labels attached to each child. "Helmsley, go over to that ticket booth, and I want Scarborough to gather near those metal stairs – there'll be quite a few o' you lot going there wi' me today."

"That's us," Sam said, double-checking Lily's label. He grabbed her cold hand and began to ease them both through the crowds. "Come on, and stay close."

Some of the other women were holding up cards, now, with the names of towns handwritten across them. Sam spotted the one for Scarborough and followed a stream of children who were heading towards it.

Their labels were checked before they were shoved towards a flight of metal platform stairs. On the opposite tracks, a train much smaller than the one they had arrived on belched smoke up towards the roof.

"Stay still!" the woman with the card ordered. She was younger than Mrs Scales but her face was wrinkled with stress and her voice was sharp. "I need to count you all, an' I can't do that unless you stop shufflin' around."

It seemed that counting was done differently in Yorkshire. In London, people mostly used numbers. Here, the woman counted by slapping each child on the top of their head.

"Hey!"

"Ouch."

"That hurt!"

Eventually, the woman stopped slapping the children and nodded to Mrs Scales. "One hundred an' eight. That's the lot of 'em." The two women exchanged relieved smiles before the one with the board pointed up the platform steps.

"Alright, you lot, follow Missus Scales!" The metal steps rang like out-of-tune bells as the group began its climb. "There's another train waiting on Platform Three to take you to Scarborough."

"I don't like this," Lily told Sam as she squeezed his hand tightly. "Why is everyone so unfriendly?"

"Don't worry, Lil," Sam said. "It'll be different when we get to Scarborough. I'm sure it'll be more organised... and nicer."

"I dunno, Sam. I don't think they like us up here. It feels like they don't really want us."

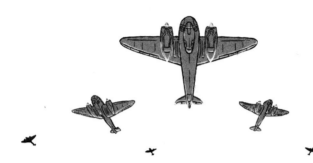

Chapter Five
Hoping for Fewer

Unsurprisingly, the train journey from York to Scarborough was much more subdued. Hardly anybody dared to speak and the overbearing presence of Mrs Scales kept even the rowdiest boys in check.

Sam and Lily spent the majority of the sixty-minute journey gazing out across the beautiful, rolling countryside. It was mostly farmers' fields and lush, green woodland. Harvest time was still a month away and golden swathes of sun-ripened wheat rippled like water in the breeze.

"I didn't know that Yorkshire was so pretty," Lily admitted. "Shame the people aren't as nice as the scenery."

"They won't all be like Missus Scales," Sam promised. "We have people much worse than her in London. I bet we'll be staying with the nicest family you can imagine."

Lily's eyes lingered on a flock of fluffy sheep munching happily in a field. "I suppose anywhere is better than staying with Missus Scales."

The children never got as far as Scarborough. Instead, their train pulled up at a pokey, red-brick station in a town called Filey. A group of stern-faced locals were waiting on the platform to meet them.

Once the children had been hustled into groups and silenced with sharp hisses, Mrs Scales stepped towards the oldest of the locals. He was wearing the nicest suit, and the serious expression on his face made Sam think that he might be in charge.

"How many this time?" the man asked.

"One 'undred an' eight," Mrs Scales answered.

"All of 'em, then." The man did nothing to disguise his obvious disappointment. "I was hoping for fewer."

Mrs Scales gave him a dismissive shrug. "The families will take 'em, Councillor Bentley. Lord knows we all need t' extra money and t' food. The rations Churchill's mob give us are nowhere near enough to see us through t' week. I don't know what they eat down in Westminster but they should try feedin' a family of 'ungry farmers."

The councillor's tight-lipped scowl suggested that he had little patience for the woman's complaints. "Some of us manage better than others, Belinda. Now, let's get this lot across to t' town hall before half of the families 'ave second thoughts."

*

Even with the tables and chairs moved into other rooms, the town hall's council chamber room was too small to comfortably house one hundred and eight children plus the large group of local mothers, but that didn't stop Mrs Scales from trying.

"Come on," she urged. "I 'ear London's streets are crowded – you lot should be used to squeezin' together."

Tom Mahoney shuffled close to Sam and Lily. "Maybe someone should remind her that half of the population have gone off to war." He glowered across at the large Yorkshire woman. "If my mum was here right now, she'd give her what for."

"If my mum was here, I'd ask her to take me straight home," Lily added.

"Hush at the back," ordered Councillor Bentley. "The sooner we get started, the sooner we get finished. We've a lot o' children to find 'omes for –" He checked his watch with a frown. "– an' it's already later than I'd like."

The mood in the crowded room was tense. The two groups faced each other like rival war clans, each eyeing the other with a mixture of curiosity and resentment. Smiles were certainly in short supply.

If the children had expected the selection process to be well organised, they were disappointed. It quickly became obvious that the local officials and Mrs Scales were making things up as they went along. Rather than adopting any carefully thought-out or fair procedure, the town's parents were simply being allowed to pick whichever children they wanted.

"I'm lookin' for two brothers," one of the women said as she prowled up and down the front row of children. "Nowt too young, mind. I want strong arms... I'm not 'ere to mollycoddle anyone."

Several pairs of brothers reluctantly raised their arms and, after assessing each one, the woman dragged the largest two from the crowd. She signed her name on a piece of paper before being handed two small boxes packed with rations: a box for each child.

Thankfully, not all of the Yorkshire mothers were as mean-spirited. Many seemed to feel genuinely sorry for the children and wrapped them in warm hugs as they escorted them to their temporary now homes. Some had even had the foresight to bring handkerchiefs to dab away tears. One or two delved into the ration boxes to hand their new charges a chunky bar of chocolate or a packet of biscuits.

Soon, only a handful of children remained. Sam and Lily were among them.

"I've only got room for one," an older woman said, stepping forward. She looked as though she was probably somebody's grandmother. "I'd prefer a girl – I had two daughters so I'm used to looking after girls."

Mrs Scales dragged a timid-looking six-year-old from the middle of the group. She had to prize the pigtailed girl's fingers from the clutch of her best friend's hand.

"No!" the girl objected. "I want to stay with my friend! Mummy promised."

"Mummy's not 'ere, is she?" Mrs Scales sneered, shoving the youngster towards the old woman. "You'd better get used to bein' on your own."

The little girl's pitiful sobs and wails could be heard from the street outside as the last few mothers made their selections. Eventually, a young woman with kind, brown eyes and carefully arranged, sandy curls pointed towards Sam.

"I'll take this boy. He has a kind face."

Sam felt his throat suddenly tighten as Lily's arm wrapped around his like an octopus' tentacle. Clearing his throat with a cough, Sam said, "We're together."

Mrs Scales snatched the list of names and signatures from the desk. "Name?"

"Sam... Samuel Hunt."

"And the girl?"

"Lily," Sam replied.

Silence hung in the air like a claustrophobic cloud as Mrs Scales ran her gaze up and down the tatty sheet. Finally, she lifted her eyes and stared triumphantly at the two children. "There's no Lily Hunt listed 'ere."

"My name's Lily Taylor," Lily explained. "We're cousins."

"I only agreed to take the one," Sam's potential host began, "but I suppose..."

"Nonsense, Missus Ward!" Mrs Scales silenced the smaller woman with a raised hand. "Cousins aren't siblings. It's 'ard enough findin' room for brothers an' sisters. If we start agreein' to find shared accommodation for every Tom, Dick an' Lily, we'll 'ave chaos on our hands."

Sam took a deep breath and stepped in front of his cousin. "I'm going nowhere without my Lily." He could feel his heart drumming against his chest as he locked icy stares with Mrs Scales. "You can send us both back to London if you want. We'll take our chances with Hitler's bombs."

"Send you back to London?" Mrs Scales took a heavy step towards him. When she leaned down close, her sour breath made Sam wince. "An' who d'you suppose will fork out for t' train fare? Your tight-fisted mothers? They've barely sent enough money to pay for board an' lodgin's."

Before he could react, the large woman reached out and wrapped her strong fingers around Sam's lapel. He felt his feet momentarily leave the ground as he was swung away from Lily and propelled towards Mrs Ward. He landed in a winded heap at the feet of the sandy-haired woman. A mixture of shock and pain welded him to the spot as Mrs Scales closed her fingers tightly around Lily's arm.

"I'll take this one 'ome wi' me!" she gloated, grinning unkindly at Sam. "We've got a spare room up at t' farm, and lots o' ways to make sure cousin Lily 'ere earns 'er keep."

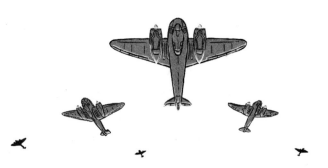

Chapter Six
Riding to Muston

The first thing that Sam had noticed about life in Filey was the air. It rolled in, unseen, across the glittering North Sea, reaching into the streets and narrow ginnels to caress everything that it touched. After just four days in his new home, Sam could feel his lungs being cleansed of London's dust and grime with every deep breath that he took. The air felt so crisp and clean that standing in Mrs Ward's clifftop garden and filling his chest had become a morning addiction. Even the squawking seagulls were beginning to recognise him.

"It won't run out, you know."

Sam didn't need to turn round to know that his

47

host was standing in the garden behind him.

Mrs Ward was a kind woman who worked in Filey's post office. She had welcomed Sam into her house like an aunt and had made him feel wanted. Part of her own morning ritual was to hang the damp washing out on a thin clothesline which stretched from one corner of her garden to the next. Sam often helped her.

"I like the way it tastes," he told Mrs Ward.

"Don't be silly, Samuel," she laughed, passing him a handful of wooden pegs and a couple of his freshly washed shirts. "Air doesn't taste of anything."

"Yes it does," Sam insisted. He hadn't yet told Mrs Ward that only his mother and aunt ever called him Samuel. He was still unsure whether or not he would ever correct her. He quite liked the familiarity. "I can taste the sea."

Mrs Ward kept smiling. "What does the air taste like in London?"

Sam was surprised by how hard he had to think.

He'd been away from home for less than a week, yet the memories of London were already fading.

"People, horses... and old dirt." He drew thick tendrils of salty air through both nostrils. "And the morning after the bombs have fallen, you can usually smell the smoke."

Mrs Ward landed a hand gently onto his shoulder. "Well, you're safe from all that 'ere. I've written to your mother to tell her 'ow well you've settled in. An' I've told her you're happy here. That's true, isn't it?"

The question surprised him. It wasn't something that he'd really thought about. War had taught him to take one day at a time and to just get on with things. It seemed that nobody thought much about being happy anymore. War wasn't a happy thing.

"I dunno," he said. "I'm not unhappy. But I miss my mum. I hope she's safe."

"Yesterday's Daily Express said the bombing has eased off a little," Mrs Ward assured him. "Mister Churchill says fewer bombers 'ave been getting through."

Sam forced himself to smile. "Do you think Lily's happy?"

He felt Mrs Ward's hand leave his shoulder as she focused on hanging out the remaining garments. When they had filled the clothesline, she took back the remaining wooden pegs.

"I'm sorry, Samuel."

"For what?"

Her sigh sounded heavy. "For not tryin' harder to take Lily. I 'ave the room and my 'enry always said we should try for a daughter... havin' Lily stay would've been good practice."

It had taken Sam a little while to work out the name of Mrs Ward's husband. Everyone in Yorkshire seemed to leave the letter H out of their words, and only when Sam had seen his name stitched into his slippers in the sitting room had he understood. Henry Ward had enlisted right before moving into Filey with his new wife. Mrs Ward had been forced to move into the cottage alone and take on work to pay the rent – though, she said, working at the post office meant that she received Henry's letters as soon as they arrived.

Sam shrugged and looked out over the garden fence, watching sunlight glinting on the sea as though it were made of diamonds.

"Missus Scales can be an intimidating woman," his host continued, twirling her long fingers around a delicate, gold chain which poked out through the neck of her blouse, "an' I didn't know 'ow I'd cope with another new person in t' house. All this is strange for us, too."

Sam had never even considered that. Guilt coloured his cheeks.

"Why don't you go an' see her?"

"Lily?" Sam was shocked. While Mrs Ward often trusted Sam to stay in the house or play on the beach while she worked or ran errands in town of an evening, so far, the London children had been forbidden from leaving Filey. Councillor Bentley had insisted that they all stay close to home, to help the settling-in process.

"O' course," said Mrs Ward. "I 'ave to go to work, now, anyway. Besides, families are important, especially in times like these." Her smile was warm and her brown eyes shone kindly. "There's a bicycle in t' shed; I'll go an' get it for you."

Outside, Mrs Ward wheeled a large bicycle out of the shed, locking the door behind her. The bicycle had seen better years but Sam wasn't about to complain.

"Now, it might be a touch too big, but I'm sure you'll get used to it," Mrs Ward said as Sam grabbed hold of the handlebars.

"Where will I find her?" Sam asked. He hadn't seen Lily on any of the short visits he'd made into Filey's compact town centre. None of the other children had seen her, either.

"Don't worry, Samuel. She hasn't vanished," Mrs Ward assured him. "Missus Scales and 'er 'usband own a farm in Muston. It's a few miles away, at the end of t' next village. The road out of Filey takes you straight past their wheat fields. I'll make you a nice 'um butty for your lunch and then you can be on your way."

"Are you sure it's OK?" Sam paused. "I thought we couldn't leave Filey."

Mrs Ward's reassuring wink sent a flutter of excitement rumbling through Sam's belly. "I won't tell if you don't," she said.

*

Sam was used to seeing soldiers – London's streets were full of them. Yet even he was surprised by the number of military vehicles and personnel that he saw on the road outside the seaside town. Most of them seemed to belong to the RAF. None of them seemed particularly pleased to be sharing the tarmac with him.

"Get off t' road!" one driver hollered from a noisy Land Rover. Several more hooted their horns as Sam tried to steer his bicycle safely. Mrs Ward had been correct: the bicycle was too big for him. It was heavy, too, which made it difficult to control, especially up steep hills.

Eventually, a troop carrier pulled over in front of him, piled high with what looked like stacks of mattresses. The engine belched thick, black diesel fumes as the driver sprang out of its cab. Sam swallowed hard as the soldier marched towards him; the pistol slung in a holster around the man's waist was an intimidating sight.

Stepping directly into Sam's path, the soldier raised his flat palm. "Stop right there!"

Sam tugged on the stiff brake and wobbled his bicycle to a squealing halt. The soldier glared at him suspiciously. "Is this your bicycle?"

"Uh, no. I mean, yes," Sam spluttered. "I've borrowed it."

"It's too big for you," the soldier observed. "If you keep riding like you have been, you'll end up getting yourself killed. We've got more important things to worry about than trying to avoid silly children, you know."

"Sorry." Sam looked down at the road, hiding from the soldier's angry eyes as he climbed off the bicycle.

"Where are you heading?" the soldier asked. His tone had softened slightly.

"Muston. It's not far..." Sam had passed a road sign a few turns earlier. Muston had only been one mile away. "I'll walk the rest of the way."

"No, you won't." The soldier grabbed the bicycle's handlebars and firmly pulled it away from Sam. He lifted it above his head as if the heavy iron bicycle was made from cardboard and slid it into the back of his truck, wedging it between two stacks of mattresses. "Get in the front – I'll drop you off."

Once they were driving, the soldier had to yell to make himself heard above the rattling engine. "You don't sound like you're from around these parts. Are you one of those evacuee kids?"

Sam nodded.

"Sounds like you're from London," the soldier continued, "like me." When Sam turned to look at him, the man was smiling. "Nice to hear a familiar accent?"

Sam nodded again.

"I'm from Highbury," the soldier told him. "You'll get used to all this peace and quiet. And the space, too."

The empty fields and hedges rolling past his window reminded Sam how different the Yorkshire countryside was to the bustling streets of London.

"The people aren't so bad, either," the soldier assured him, "once you get used to them." The truck's engine rumbled noisily, rattling the bare metal floor beneath Sam's feet as the vehicle roared into Muston.

The soldier slowed his truck as the narrow road sent them weaving through a cluster of cottages and terraces. As they passed a church, he asked, "Where do you want dropping off?"

"Is there a farm in the village?"

The soldier nodded. His face creased as if he'd just sucked a slice of raw lemon. "It's run by the Scales family. Why do you want to go there?"

"My cousin Lily is staying with them."

"Well, I hope she likes hard work," the soldier said, shaking his head as he slowed the truck to a standstill. He pointed to a large iron gate sitting at the entrance to what appeared to be a private road. "From what I've heard, Scales Farm makes those old Victorian workhouses look like luxury hotels."

Sam felt like somebody had just punched him in the stomach as he climbed out of the truck's cabin. He walked round to the driver's door to find the soldier leaning through the open window.

"I'll keep the bicycle for now."

"But..."

The man smiled. "Don't worry, you can have it back. But I'd rather you walked home – there's less chance of you having an accident."

"How will I get it back?"

"Come to the RAF base at Hunmanby Moor," the man told him. Then, seeing the bewildered expression on Sam's face, he laughed. "It's only a couple of miles down the road from Filey. It's where a bloke called Butlin will be opening a holiday camp when this damn war is over. If I'm not there, I'll be at St. Margaret's Primary School in the village. We've commandeered it for extra billets and we move an entire company of two hundred men in on Thursday. I'm on mattress transport duty. Ask for Corporal Timmins."

Before driving away, Corporal Timmins fixed Sam with a concerned gaze. "I hope your cousin is all right." He switched his attention to the heavy gate and pulled his lips tight. "It's true, you know – you really do find out what people are like during wars."

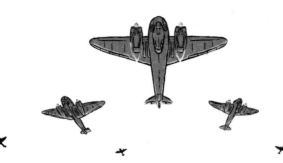

Chapter Seven
Screams at Scales Farm

The roughly painted sign tacked to the rusted iron gate confirmed that the property was Scales Farm. The scribbled words *'Keep Out'* made it clear that uninvited visitors were definitely not welcome, but Sam wasn't about to let a couple of words intimidate him, nor would he let them prevent him from checking on Lily. He just decided to make his house call in a more covert fashion.

The farm itself appeared to be surrounded on three sides by fields of wheat and barley. Even though the crops hadn't yet been harvested, they offered Sam very little camouflage. The swaying stems hardly reached up to his chest and, even if he stooped, he would still be in clear view from the windows of the grey, stone farmhouse in the distance.

To the left of the property and its outbuildings, perhaps shielding the buildings from the fierce winter gales and storms, sat a dense stretch of woodland. Once inside the first row of trees, Sam found that he could easily navigate his way from the road to the house completely unseen.

He'd only taken a few dozen steps inside the woods when the gentle rustling of leaves and the tweeting of birds were disturbed by a piercing scream. Raised hairs prickled the back of Sam's neck as he realised that it was a sound that he had heard before. The scream belonged to Lily.

With his senses suddenly on high alert, Sam

scanned the scrum of tree trunks for any sign of his cousin, but the only movement came from the dashing of a squirrel as it moved from one tree to another.

He was still moving forwards when the next scream reached him through the forest, this time even louder and closer. Lily was moving towards him. Feeling disoriented and exposed, Sam threw his desperate gaze from left to right. He bounced from one tree trunk to the next, trying to work out where the screams were coming from. However, it wasn't Lily's third and final scream that filled Sam's limbs with adrenaline – it was the cruel howls and whoops of laughter that followed close behind it.

His younger cousin was being hunted.

Now, he could hear the crashing and thumping of panic-stricken footsteps as they raced through the forest towards him. Flashes of movement caught his eye and he followed the brief swishes of red hair until he finally caught sight of Lily sidestepping between the trees.

His cousin's terrified sobs guided Sam forwards

until Lily burst from between two narrow trunks and crashed straight into him. Luckily, Sam anticipated the impact. He met his cousin with a textbook rugby tackle, wrapping her in a protective embrace before throwing them both into a thick nest of bronzing bracken leaves. Just as Lily was about to scream again, Sam clamped his hand across her mouth and whispered into her ear, "Shh. It's me, Lils. I'm here."

Close by, heavy footsteps clattered towards them. The catcalls of two loud males meant that his cousin's pursuers were close. Lily huddled against him, shaking like a feral creature. They both squirmed deep into the bracken, wriggling between and beneath the heavy russet leaves.

"Don't let them find me," Lily whispered.

The two cousins held their breath as twin sets of footsteps drew closer and closer. When four heavy boots thumped to a standstill inches from the Londoners' heads, Sam could smell the damp mud on the closest boot's sole.

"We know you're 'ere!" a growling voice called. "Our ma's gonna be madder than a rabid dog if we're not all back for lunch."

"Aye," boomed a second voice, this one even deeper and more unfriendly than the first. "There's chores to do, and you're gonna cop it for keepin' us out. You're already in Ma's bad books for bein' a lazy scrounger."

Sam felt his cousin's body tighten with anger. His voice was barely louder than a breath as he whispered into Lily's ear. "Don't say anything. They'll never find us."

The two hunters stood their ground, clearly listening for any sounds of movement. When none came, the owner of the deepest voice broke the silence.

"Daft mare 'as probably made 'er way back to t' farm."

"Maybe," agreed his companion. "Or p'raps she's done a runner. Our ma'll tear 'er guts out if she's tried to find that cousin of 'ers."

Both sets of feet started to move away, kicking their way through the bracken and snapping twigs. Sam kept his younger cousin locked in his embrace until the footsteps had padded away into silence. Only then did the children scramble to their feet.

"Who were they?" Sam asked.

Lily brushed leaves and twigs from her clothes. "Vincent and Duncan. They're brothers."

"Why are they looking for you?"

"So they can throw me in the manure heap."

"The *what*?"

Lily shrugged. "They take deliveries from other farms. It's to spread on the wheat fields during autumn."

"But why would they want to throw you in all that... stuff?"

"'Cause they're bullies," Lily said, "and nobody will stop them."

Sam helped his cousin climb free of the bracken

leaves. "What about Missus Scales? Doesn't she stop them?"

"Ha!" Lily sneered. "She's worse than they are. If that wicked woman had her way, I'd live in the barn with the chickens. She treats me worse than one of her dogs."

Sam could feel rage boiling a red rash across his neck. He clenched his fists tight. "I'm sorry, Lils. I didn't know."

"It's not your fault."

Sam shook his head. "I should have come sooner. I'm supposed to be looking after you."

"No, Sam, you're not," Lily told him. "That's supposed to be Missus Scales' job. But she seems to think I'm here to work for her, instead."

Sam remembered one of the Scales boys mentioning something about chores. That wasn't supposed to be part of the deal. They'd come north to find sanctuary, not slavery.

"You're not going back," he insisted. "Missus

Ward's a kind woman. She'll take you in, I'm sure."

"Missus Scales will never agree to it," Lily said, sadly. "She'll never give up the allowance and extra rations – even though I never see any of them."

"But that food is meant for you!" Sam said, shocked. "It's why Aunt Peg sends the money every week."

Lily looked down at her scuffed shoes. "Well, it's being used to feed those boys of hers. I'm lucky if I get to eat their leftovers." Her eyes flicked up towards Sam, gazing across at him with sudden hope. "Do you have any food on you, Sam? I'm starving."

Sam dug into his pockets, eventually pulling out the remains of the half-eaten ham sandwich that Mrs Ward had given him earlier. He was still trying to peel away the paper that it was wrapped in when Lily snatched it from his fingers. His jaw dropped open as he watched his cousin devour it in two huge bites. Her cheeks bulged as she chewed hungrily.

"Can you bring more?" Lily asked. "Anything will do."

"Come back with me, now," Sam said. "I'll ask Missus Ward to cook you something nice for lunch. You can have my rations."

Lily glanced over her shoulder, in the direction of the farmhouse. Fear wrapped itself around her face like a mask. "I can't. Missus Scales expects me back to clean the stairs." She rubbed her arm and winced as if it was tender. "I'm already in enough trouble."

"You must get some time to yourself."

Lily nodded. "Maybe later, around three? It's ration day and Missus Scales wants me to collect this week's food from Filey."

"That's it, then," Sam said. "I'll meet you outside the gates at three."

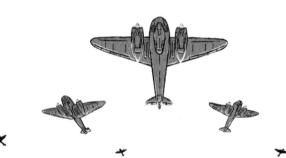

Chapter Eight
Lucky for Some

A copper bell jangled feebly above their heads as Sam and Lily entered Hargraves' grocery store. The shop was surprisingly quiet and when the smiling shopkeeper waved a customer goodbye, the two children found that they had the shop to themselves.

"I've got my eye on you two," the large man warned them. A round belly strained to escape through a white apron tied around the man's thick waist. Sunlight bounced off his balding scalp as he winked at them. "I close in an hour, so don't you be dawdlin'."

Lily drew near to her cousin as she stared at a lightly stocked shelf. Trays of fresh eggs seemed to gaze back at her like bulging eyes. Beside them, hunks of cheese and butter rested on cold plates. Another shelf held staples like sugar, tea and small pots of fruit jams.

Both children resisted the urge to reach out and snatch a pot for themselves. It had been months since they'd tasted anything as delicious as sweet, sticky jam. Sam heard Lily's stomach groaning noisily and he wondered if his cousin was imagining feasting on buttered toast and strawberry preserve.

Sam could feel his cheeks tingling as his mind conjured up similar thoughts. He stared longingly at a stack of freshly sliced bacon rashers, remembering how his mum used to fry his until they were crispy and then pack four at a time into his Sunday morning breakfast sandwiches. Times had certainly changed since Hitler had sent his stormtroopers marching across Europe.

"The shelves look half empty," Lily whispered. "I thought things were bad in London but there's hardly anything here."

As if sensing his young customer's concerns, the shopkeeper leaned against his countertop. Light from the bulb hanging from the ceiling bounced off his pink scalp as he said, "It's been a busy day. I haven't had time to restock t' shelves."

"Should we come back tomorrow?" Sam asked.

"No, no, no. Don't be daft, lad," the shopkeeper laughed. "If you can't see what you need on those shelves, I'll have it in t' back. It's my name on the front, so I make sure folk around here can count on me. Who are you shopping for?"

Sam nudged his cousin.

"Oh, uh, Missus Scales. From the..."

The smile faded from Mr Hargraves' lips. "Scales Farm? Aye, I know it well." His cheeks wobbled as he blew out a mouthful of air. "There's a lot o' mouths to feed down there... you're going to clean me out. CONNIE?" He shouted this last word, causing both children to jump. A few seconds later, a large, pleasant-looking woman in a cream apron appeared through the back doorway of the shop, wearing an inquisitive expression. She was followed by a tall, surly-looking teenage boy.

"Did you bring t' book?" the man asked Lily.

Lily delved into her pocket to retrieve a small, creased Ministry of Food ration book. It was identical to the one owned by her mother, right down to the two sharp staples holding the thin sheets in place.

She handed it to the shopkeeper, who immediately turned to a large ledger resting beside his till. He ran a finger down a list of handwritten names, pausing only when he had almost reached the bottom.

"They certainly like their grub down on Scales Farm," he grumbled. He squinted at what looked like a fresh entry. "Two growin' boys an' that lodger o' theirs. Says 'ere there's one of them evacuees staying with them, now, an' all. I guess that'll be one of you?"

Lily nodded slowly.

Mr Hargraves' wife gazed at her gently and

smiled. "Aye, nothing lasts forever, lass. This war'll be over in a jiffy, an' then you can go back down to London."

"If there's anything left of it," Sam said.

Both children jumped again as Mr Hargraves slammed a large cardboard packing box down onto the wooden countertop. "Hey, we'll have none of that talk in my shop. Our lads are gonna give Jerry a right good 'iding, just you wait an' see."

He snatched up the ration book and opened it wide. "Now then, let's get this show on t' road. I always start with t' eggs. One each per week. I'll let you bring 'em to me."

For the next ten minutes, the shopkeeper directed both children and the teenage boy around his store like a skilled puppet master. "Five lots of butter," he told Sam, pointing at the shelf. "Two ounces each. And bring me five four-ounce packets of margarine, too – that's on the shelf below."

Lily was given similar instructions. Five lots of everything: ten ounces of sugar, five portions of cheese and more bottles of milk than either of the children had seen in a long time.

"Are you sure this is right?" Lily asked, putting the last of the fifteen pints of milk on the shopkeeper's counter. Sam wondered how she was going to get it all back to Scales Farm.

"Aye, love," Mr Hargraves nodded kindly. "Three pints each. It's not a lot when you think about it, especially when it's got to last an entire week. I 'ave to limit myself to two cups o' tea a day, otherwise me missus 'ere complains there's not enough for 'er weekly baking." He rubbed his stomach. "An' we can't be 'avin that!"

To collect the final item, Lily had to ask Sam to pull a packet of dried egg powder from the shop's highest shelf. Behind them, the shopkeeper was busy dropping thin, four-ounce packages of rationed bacon and ham into their box. Each one offered barely enough protein to fill a sandwich. However, despite the paltry portions, Mrs Scales' rations still seemed to be adding up.

As the grocer's wife reached under his counter, she told the children, "Now, I know that Missus Scales always likes her fresh oranges. Trouble is, since those Jerry submarines started blockin' our convoys, oranges 'ave become a bit scarce." She gently placed a small paper bag onto the countertop. "But some clever farmers over in Wales 'ave started growing blackcurrants. We've got plenty o' these, now, so tell Missus Scales I've popped a bag in the box to see 'ow she likes 'em."

As Sam gazed at the box filled with food, he began to understand why Mrs Scales was so keen to host an evacuee. Mr Hargraves had mentioned a lodger, too. More people meant more rations. Lucky for some!

Mr Hargraves scribbled a final row of crosses in the ration book coupons to show that Mrs

Scales had received her full quota for the week. When he had closed the book and his ledger, Lily reached back into her pocket and opened her mouth to speak. To Sam's surprise, the teenage boy who had been helping them to collect the items cut her off.

"I'll show you out," he said, and he scooped up the box of rations and carried it towards the door, ushering Lily ahead of him.

The bell jangled overhead again and they squinted against the sunlight as the door closed behind them. The street was quiet, but the tall teenager looked up and down it carefully before leading Sam and Lily round the back of the shop. Here, a rusting old bicycle was leaning against the brickwork with a basket affixed to the handlebars. In a low voice, he asked, "Did, uh... did Missus Scales give you owt else?"

Bemused, Sam stared from the boy to his cousin. Lily, however, nodded. She dipped her fingers into her pocket and fished out a crumpled, brown envelope.

The boy opened it up and read the small letter

inside. A single banknote was pinned to one corner. He nodded silently, before creasing the note into his pocket and reaching into the basket on the front of his bicycle. "You 'aven't seen this, right?"

"Seen what?" Sam asked.

The boy winked. "That's the idea. I like a fast learner."

As Sam and Lily swapped befuddled shrugs, the boy pulled two bulging packages from the basket. Each was wrapped in brown paper and the corner of the largest dripped with what might have been blood. The end of a thick sausage pierced the corner of the smaller package.

"Hey! That's not part of rationing," Sam pointed out. "At least not where we come from."

The boy scowled and put a finger to his lips. "This is what we like t' call *black-market portions*. I don't ask where t' butchers get their spare meat from, and they don't ask who I sell it to while I'm on my deliveries. That way, everyone's 'appy."

Sam felt a familiar tingle as his mouth began to water. "I haven't had sausages in months."

The boy smiled wryly. "You can 'ave as much as you want – as long as you've got the money."

"I thought there was meant to be a food shortage!" said Lily.

He laughed sharply. "Aye, and there are fairies hidden at the bottom of some folk's gardens, too."

Lily's eyes widened. "Really?"

"Of course not," said the tall teenager, rolling his eyes. "But if you believe everyone has to go wi'out during rationing, you might as well believe in those fairies."

"You should try living down in London," Sam told him, pointing at the box of rations. "My mum says knitting mist is easier than making our rations last a week."

The boy tapped the end of his nose. "But I'll wager t' rich folk in t' fancy London houses don't 'ave to go 'ungry. You don't think 'is Majesty and

Mister Churchill's government are scratching by on one egg a week like the rest o' us, d'you?"

"But that's not fair," Sam complained. "While us normal folk starve, others still have full plates?"

"Aye, and life's always been like that," said the boy, hauling the box of rations onto the back of his bicycle and securing it. "But who says any o' us 'ave to starve?"

Sam stared back at him. "The government? Aren't they the ones who introduced rationing?"

"Rationing is there to control the food we're allowed to *buy*," the teenager continued. "But there's nowt to say you can't grow your own food, too. Why d'you think there are no flowers in any of t' gardens up 'ere? Everyone's dug 'em up to grow their own crops."

"There aren't many gardens in London," Lily lamented.

Sam nodded in agreement. "Not where we live, anyway."

"But we're not in London, are we?" said the boy, swinging his leg over his bicycle. "We're in good old, bountiful Yorkshire, an' that means there are fields and woodlands and even the sea. An' all o' them are like a generous larder o' free nosh. You just need to know 'ow and where to get your hands on it."

Chapter Nine
Free Time in Filey

The boy seemed eager to deliver the groceries to Scales Farm himself. Sam wondered if that was because he'd be picking up another banknote for his troubles.

Lily didn't seem to care. Sam could see that his cousin was just happy not to have to cart the heavy box of rations back herself. Her hosts hadn't volunteered any money for bus fare and there was no way that Lily would have been able to carry all of that food alone. This meant that she now had some unexpected free time, and her constant grin told Sam that she was looking forward to sharing that with him.

"Can we go to the beach?" she asked. "I heard

the two brothers talking about a mile of sand." Her eyes widened at the thought. "What do you think a mile of sand even looks like?"

Sam didn't tell Lily that he'd already seen the beach, several times in fact. Nor did he tell her that, if the waves hadn't made their way back up the beach yet, he'd be able to show her the footprints that he'd pressed into the sand before breakfast.

"Auntie Joan always said the sea air was good for you," Lily reminded him.

Sam grinned as he thought about his mother. "Yeah, but she also says that Pontefract cakes can cure stomach ache, and those things are disgusting!"

As the thought of those small liquorice sweets screwed up Lily's face, Sam grabbed her hand. "OK, I'll take you to the beach," he said. "But I want you to meet Missus Ward first."

"No, Sam," Lily objected, dipping her head to remind him how shy she was. "Another time?"

"Now," Sam insisted, tugging her gently. "You need a good, square meal, and Missus Ward will love meeting you."

The thought of a plate of freshly cooked food quickly drained any reluctance from Lily's feet. In seconds, the two children were sprinting down Filey's high street, laughing as though worry and fear had both been abolished forever.

Filey's quaint village streets felt almost deserted. A hodge-podge of white and cream, two and three-storey buildings lined the main shopping street, seated atop glass shopfronts like a family set of crowns. As Sam stared up at the uneven mixture of gables and chimneys and turret-framed rooftops, Lily busied herself with peering into the shops themselves. The window displays were sparse, perhaps reflecting the country's current lack of consumer appetite. After all, most people had better things to do with their time and money than shop.

It was mid-afternoon and if Sam and Lily had been in London, they would have been navigating their way through throngs of fellow Londoners. Today, though, they seemed to have the small seaside town almost all to themselves.

"It's like a ghost town," Lily whispered. "Where is everyone?"

Sam shrugged his shoulders as the screech of rooftop seagulls made him think back to the air raid sirens of home. "Maybe this is what towns are like outside London. I quite like it – don't you?"

Now, it was Lily's turn to twitch her shoulders. "I dunno. I think I prefer it when there are lots of other people around."

It was the rattle of laughter that made Lily feel more at ease. A trio of young mothers burst out of a bric-a-brac shop, pulling squabbling toddlers behind them like dogs on leads. The group gave Sam and Lily a curious glance as they bustled past.

Across the road, a couple of pensioners emerged from the doorway of a pub. Tendrils of smoke reached after them, filling the air with the bitter scent of pipe tobacco. As if on cue, more people joined them, spilling from a small tea room and the cobbler's.

Sam sighed, as though having to share the town with other inhabitants was a disappointment. At the end of the street, the post office came into view and he quickened his footsteps, his rumbling belly suddenly reminding him that he was hungry. His mind was busily teasing his tastebuds with enticing thoughts of what Mrs Ward might make for dinner, so it was quite a shock when he was abruptly bundled through the archway of a damp and dingy alley.

"Hey!" he gasped, as his shoulder thumped against a stone column.

"Shh!" Lily ordered, pinning her cousin to the dirty wall. "He might see us."

The fear in his cousin's voice sent adrenaline flushing through Sam's body. "Who?"

Still welding Sam to the brickwork with her right arm, Lily stretched to peer back out into the high street. Her head jerked left, then right. When she returned her attention to Sam, both eyes were wide with fear. "It's Missus Scales' lodger."

"Who is he?"

"Some guy called Albert, or Alfred. No, Albert." Lily shuffled uncomfortably, hugging her own shoulders. "He gives me the creeps. He comes and goes at really strange times; I hardly see him. I can smell his disgusting cigarettes, though."

"But why are we hiding?"

Lily's eyes didn't leave the street. "If he sees me here with you, he might tell Missus Scales."

Sam rubbed his aching shoulder. "You aren't doing anything wrong, Lils."

"That doesn't matter," Lily hissed. "I don't want him to see me." She screwed her face into a map of wrinkles. "He skulks around and doesn't really speak to anyone. It's as if he's more important than everyone else, and I'm pretty sure he hates the sight of me."

Sam tightened his lips. He knew better than to argue with Lily when his cousin was so worked up. Instead, he edged along the brickwork until his chin hovered above his cousin's shoulder.

"Is that him?"

Lily's gaze was glued to a tall, dark-haired man who was standing in the high street, speaking in an undertone to the town's vicar. Lily nodded, and they both furtively watched Albert bid the vicar goodbye and make his way down the town's high street. Strong, handsome features and sharp cheekbones made the man look impressive and at well over six feet tall, he was difficult to miss. He wore a stylish, grey, buttoned-up jacket and black hat, which he tipped silently to the various shoppers who stopped to wish him a 'good afternoon'. Sam noticed how he weaved between groups of people in a purposeful way, as though avoiding being spoken to.

"See? Told you he was a bit shifty," Lily said. "Look at the way he walks."

Sam looked. It was true; Albert had a stiff way of moving around which made him look uneasy and haughty. Sam heard the worry in Lily's voice and tried to reassure her. "He's just doing his shopping, Lils," he said. "And people seem to like him."

They both continued to watch in silence, tracking Albert's every move as he navigated the gentle curve of the road towards the seafront. Sam was about to tell Lily that the lodger was clearly just intent on taking a stroll along the beach when a gaggle of noisy, chatting women rounded the corner and Albert made a sudden detour down a side street.

"See what I mean?" Lily asked. "Weird, or what?"

"Lily, he hasn't done anything wrong. He's just walking."

"You don't believe me, do you?" Lily looked hurt.

Seizing his cousin's hand, Sam stepped back out onto the high street. Lily seemed more comfortable, now that Albert was out of sight, but it didn't last long.

"Let's follow him," Sam insisted.

"What?" Lily snatched her hand back. "Why? No!"

Sam set off down the street backwards, his eyes fixed on Lily's horrified expression. "To show you that there's nothing to be frightened of."

Lily shook her head as if her hair were filled with fleas. "What if he sees us? He'll tell –"

"He won't see us," Sam promised. "Missus Scales will never know. And once I've shown you that there's nothing scary about him, we can go and see Missus Ward."

"You promise?"

Sam smiled. "Scout's honour!" He grabbed his cousin's hand again and tugged her across the pavement. "Come on!"

Chapter Ten
Caught in the Act

"You're not even in the Scouts," Lily reminded her cousin as they crouched behind an overgrown garden hedgerow.

Sam peered around a stone gatepost. "What?"

"You said *Scout's honour*," Lily continued, "but you've never been a Scout. You said you didn't like the neckties."

Swallowing a giggle, Sam said, "I've never played for Chelsea, either, but I can still play football if I want to." He looked back at Lily and winked. "Besides, Dad says it all the time and he's never been a Scout, either. It just means 'I promise', and I always keep those, don't I? Lils?"

Lily wasn't listening. "I can see him."

Sam had quite enjoyed tracking the lodger. They'd spent the last few minutes catching glimpses of Albert's grey clothing and flashes of his black hat as he had made his way through the town's labyrinth of squashed-in backstreets.

"What's he doing?" Lily asked wearily. It was clear that she wasn't enjoying the chase.

"I think he went down the alley behind the barber's shop." Sam moved a stray branch out of the way to get a better view of the street.

"He definitely doesn't want to be seen."

"Lily, he probably just –"

"Please, Sam," Lily groaned. "My legs are tired. Can't we stop this?"

Sam paused to study Lily's face and knelt down beside her again. "I thought you wanted to know what he was up to. I'm doing this for you."

"I did," Lily shook her head. "I do. I want you to believe me. But we're wasting time, Sam. Missus Scales will start to wonder where I am soon, and I want to see where you live."

Sam sighed. He didn't want his cousin to go back to her hosts worrying about this man when there was nothing to be afraid of.

"OK. You stay here," he told Lily. "I'll just go to the end of that alley and then come back."

Sam felt Lily's fingers grip his sleeve. "Be careful, Sam. Something about that bloke isn't right."

Lily's words were still fresh in Sam's ears as he made his way towards the mouth of the alley. Three-storey stone buildings reached up either side of the one-metre-wide channel. The lips of overhanging rooftops acted as a shield against the daylight so that when Sam began to edge his way down the alley, he quickly found himself cocooned in gloom. He blinked, feeling as though his eyes were fighting to peer through a veil. Reminded of the warehouses back home, he reached out with his hands, moving his dexterous fingers across the cold stone and mortar. He kept his eyes fixed on the bright strip of the approaching exit in front of him and when he reached it, he launched himself out into the afternoon light.

He blinked as his eyes adjusted. Squinting down the narrow street into which he had stumbled, he was met by a row of neat, terraced houses on an empty road. The only living thing in sight was a lonely seagull, which took flight the moment it saw Sam.

His quarry had vanished.

Just as Sam was preparing to turn and head back through the alley to Lily, a voice behind him turned his blood to ice.

"Why are you following me?"

Sam whipped around and instantly felt himself pulled forwards by the front of his coat. As he was pushed roughly against the cream house to one side of the alleyway, Sam took in the sight of Albert. The man's dark eyes were stretched wide with startled rage and he was sweating heavily.

Sam's words failed him; the solid stone had impacted upon his ribs like a boxer's punch, knocking the air out of his lungs. He spluttered like a fish out of water and searched all around him for any kind of response.

"*Why are you following me?*" Albert's strong hands closed even tighter around the front of Sam's clothing, dragging him up off the ground. His eyes raked Sam's face as though he were trying to read Sam's intentions through his skin.

Pain from Sam's bruised chest sent tears spilling down his cheeks as he struggled to reply. "Let... me... go..."

"Answer the question," Albert pressed him urgently, breathing hard.

Still in pain, Sam struggled to find the courage to speak. "I'll... tell the... police."

"Tell them what?" The man shook Sam as though information might rattle out of him onto the cobbles. "Answer me, boy. Tell them what?"

Not wanting to wait around to find out what

might happen next, Sam rammed his palms into Albert's chest and drove the heel of his shoe into the man's shin. He was rewarded with a shocked howl and, as instinct pushed Albert's hands towards his damaged leg, Sam managed to wriggle free.

Sam was pursued back up the alley by a torrent of threats but nothing else and, when he burst out into the blinding daylight of the street, he was alone. Sam was still gasping for breath when he reached Lily's hiding place.

"Sam! You're hurt. What happened?"

Ignoring his cousin's worried interrogation, he grabbed Lily's wrist and frantically began to pilot her towards the safety of Filey's town centre. In fact, he didn't stop running until they both rounded a corner and almost crashed straight into their school friend, Tom Mahoney.

Feeling too spooked to stop and chat with Tom, Sam continued to sprint through the town towards the beach with Lily close behind. They quickly found themselves outside a smart-looking, stone shopfront with double doors and a sign which read 'Post Office'.

"Why didn't you say something to Tom?" Lily asked as they stopped to catch their breath.

Sam hoped that his exercise-reddened cheeks disguised his embarrassment. "Say what? That I followed a complete stranger and got caught in the act? He would have said I was stupid. He'd probably say I deserved it, too."

"Tom's not like that. He's your friend," Lily insisted. "He looks up to you."

"Yeah, and that's exactly why I didn't tell him," Sam snapped. "Can we talk about it later? We're here!"

The inside of the post office was warm, shaded and pleasantly busy. Many businesses were being staffed by women during the war, and two ladies were visible behind the glossy, wooden counter but neither was Mrs Ward. One was serving a very old gentleman with a cane, who seemed to be holding out his pension book; the other was stuffing a handwritten telegram into an envelope stamped with a blue mark.

She handed it to a teenage boy, who slipped it into a bag around his middle and exited the building. Sam and Lily heard the ringing of his bicycle bell as he set off up the street towards his destination.

Lily was looking expectantly up at Sam, as though hoping to sense which woman was Mrs Ward from his expression. After a few moments, however, Sam's host bustled through from the back of the shop with a beaming smile on her face. "Samuel! What are you doing back so soon?" She didn't wait for a response. "We're closing in a minute. Are you 'ungry?"

Sam could almost hear Lily's stomach rumbling and nodded, grinning.

One of the other ladies looked up from her work and checked the clock on the wall. "You go, Vivien," she said kindly. "We'll be all right, now."

Mrs Ward smiled even more broadly and reached up into a small pigeonhole where several small parcels and letters were stacked. "Come on, then," she said, putting the mail into her bag as she swept Sam and Lily out of the post office. "'Ave a lovely evening, ladies."

*

Back in Mrs Ward's welcoming kitchen, Lily shuffled behind her cousin's shoulder as Mrs Ward stepped towards her. When the woman grabbed her wrist, Lily tried to pull away but Mrs Ward was too strong. "Come 'ere, girl. Let me 'ave a look at you." Lily whimpered a little but the young woman eased her forwards.

Tenderly, Mrs Ward pushed a stray strand of red hair back behind Lily's ear and plucked a fallen eyelash from her cheek. "You really should've told me that your cousin was so pretty." She wrapped her arms around Lily and pulled her against her chest, surrounding her with affection.

At first, Sam was pleased to see his cousin submit to the embrace but that relief instantly turned to horror when Lily began to sob. Mrs Ward pressed a kiss against Lily's head as she comforted her. "Now, now. Let's not be 'avin' tears in this house. There's nothin' but love waiting for you 'ere."

Lily buried her face into the soft fabric of Mrs Ward's dress and snaked both arms around the woman's waist.

"I'm not your mummy," Mrs Ward whispered, "but there'll always be a great big hug 'ere for you, my love. Oh, an' how about a fresh slice o' leek and potato pie? It'll still be warm."

The food was delicious. Mrs Ward filled both of their plates with a generous slice of creamy pie and then added mashed potato, crushed carrots and cabbage, all picked fresh from her own garden earlier that morning.

"I guess this is what the shop boy meant," Sam acknowledged, as his host added a fresh dollop of potato to his plate.

When he explained, Mrs Ward smiled. "The 'ole town grows its own food. Lots of folk keep chickens, for the free eggs. Old Missus Thompson even 'as a couple of breeding pigs in that big shed of 'ers," she told them. "One of the reasons I chose this 'ouse was for the smallholding. I just 'arvest the food and replant my seeds. Nature takes care of t' rest."

"What would you do if you didn't have a garden?" asked Sam as he began to eat. He cast his thoughts back to London and the tightly packed terraced streets of Bethnal Green. The only thing that ever grew in the cramped back yard of his home was the odd flowering dandelion.

His host patted a loose strand of hair back into place and set about washing some flower pots in the sink, which overlooked the garden. "I wouldn't like to think about that, Sam. The rations we get don't stretch very far. Without the extras we grow ourselves, we'd be 'ungry most days. It's not a lot, but it 'elps." She glanced out of the window before her at the shed and, sounding concerned, added, "Where's the bicycle I sent you with?"

Swallowing quickly, Sam rushed to explain that Corporal Timmins had confiscated the bicycle and that he would need to go and collect it. "If he's not at Hunmanby Moor," Sam rattled off, "he'll be at the local school."

"St. Margaret's? Why?"

In between mouthfuls, Sam explained, "They're moving soldiers in on Thursday. Two hundred, he said."

When Mrs Ward did not reply, Sam paused with his fork halfway to his mouth. "I'm sorry, Missus Ward," he said, feeling a flutter of nerves in his middle.

"Sorry?" Mrs Ward repeated, looking around. "What are you sorry for, Samuel?"

"For losing the bicycle," Sam mumbled. "I shouldn't have taken it."

"Nonsense," Mrs Ward smiled at him. "You were dyin' to see your Lily an' I'm just glad that you're safe."

Lily was shovelling pie and carrots into a mouth that was already bulging with delicious food. She chewed like she hadn't eaten in weeks.

"There's no rush, Lily," Mrs Ward giggled. "Nobody will steal your food. And you both might want to leave some space for afters."

Sam raised an eyebrow. "Afters?"

Mrs Ward dried her hands and then, with the flare of a magician's assistant, swept a tea cloth from the dish that it was covering. The smell of some freshly baked delight billowed towards them. "Rhubarb crumble."

*

Later, as they happily nursed bellies bulging with pie and crumble, Sam and Lily set off for the beach. A gate from the back garden led to a shortcut down to the beach and as Sam steered his cousin towards the narrow footpath, he suddenly paused. "Wait," he said. "I forgot something."

There was hope in Lily's voice. "More pie?"

"Only if you want to burst," Sam laughed. "No, but something just as good."

He returned several minutes later, carrying an armful of fishing rods and nets.

"I can't eat those," grumbled Lily.

Sam handed her a large pole net. "Maybe not, but we can catch things that can be eaten. How do you fancy fish pie tomorrow?"

Lily's mouth drooped as she brushed loose strands of red hair behind her ear. "Tomorrow, I'll be back on the farm, watching Vincent and Duncan fill their greedy mouths."

"Not if I have anything to do with it," Sam promised her. He closed the garden gate behind him and started down the footpath. "Come on, Lils. Let's go find ourselves some of the free nosh the shop boy was bragging about."

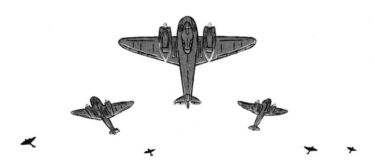

Chapter Eleven
Fishing for Free Nosh

By the time they had reached the beach, the rolling tide was beginning its slow creep back towards the cliff face. The afternoon's fading sunshine had managed to dry dappled patches of sand but, as Sam and Lily made their way towards a cluster of rock pools, their feet left a trail of damp impressions.

To their left, they could see a line of small, painted fishing boats moored on the sand at the foot of the cliff. A scruffy tidal line of flotsam, made mostly from twigs of driftwood, seaweed and torn-up fishing nets, suggested that the boats sat beyond the sea's reach. Above their heads, dusk was already beginning to win its tussle with daylight and the greying sky warned both children that evening wasn't far away.

It was Lily's first ever visit to a beach and she seemed eager to make the most of every minute. Sam was having trouble keeping up with his cousin, who raced across the sand. However, despite her clear enthusiasm, it was obvious that Lily's senses were struggling to cope with the feast of new sights and sounds and smells. The breeze whipping in from the ocean had already turned her hair into a tousled nest, and the salty aroma that it carried pulled sneezes from her nostrils.

"You'll get used to that sea air," Sam assured her.

Stretching her arms wide, Lily turned to look at her own pathway of footprints, leading back across the sand.

"This place is amazing," she gasped. "It's so... vast!"

Sam nodded. "Sure beats the slimy bank of the Thames, eh?"

A solemn look draped itself across Lily's eyes. "I wish Mum and Auntie Joan could see all this."

Sam did his best to chase her gloom away. "We'll bring them back here as soon as our boys beat Jerry." He pointed towards the cluster of dark rock pools that seemed to push through the sand like the stumps of rotten teeth. "If we're lucky, there'll be a couple of crabs, or maybe even a lobster, trapped in those waters."

Ahead of them, rising high enough to make them strain their necks, was a vast slab of ancient rock. The constant crashing and churning of the North Sea had gradually eroded the fragile cliff face elsewhere, but the darker stone of Filey's magnificent Brigg was made of sterner stuff. It stretched out into the ocean like a huge, impenetrable wall. The rock pools followed its path, lining the Brigg's shadow until the foaming sea swallowed them whole.

Sam and Lily weren't the only people hoping to harvest the rock pools. Small figures moved slowly from one rock cluster to the next, dipping their own nets. One of those figures looked familiar.

"Tom!" Sam yelled. "Tom Mahoney!"

Sam was pleased. He'd been feeling a little guilty about ignoring his friend earlier. Now, he could make up for that. The wind caught his voice and shredded it to silence but their friend didn't need to hear Sam's calls. He was already heading towards them.

"Not in as much of a hurry, now, I see," Tom joshed.

"Sorry, Tom. We were late for tea at Missus Ward's," Sam lied.

"Really?" Tom gave him a puzzled look. "Jesse Owens would have struggled to catch you two – I thought you must have been running away from something."

Lily stepped forward, eager to change the subject. "Where does all this sand come from? It's like a desert."

Tom laughed and waved his hands "I know. Look at all this space."

"It feels like we're in another country," Lily observed, biting her lip as she tried to hide a smile. Brightly flushed cheeks made it clear that she was happy to see Tom. Sam had always known that his younger cousin had a soft spot for their school friend, and seeing Lily's happiness cheered him up. From the glow on Tom's face, those feelings were mutual.

"Caught anything?" Sam asked, nodding towards the rock pools.

"Shellfish, mainly," Tom said. "A couple of clams, some mussels and an oyster, I think."

"No crabs?" Sam wondered.

"Not yet. They hide under the rocks and in the sand, so they're harder to find. Pamela thinks she's got one trapped, though."

Lily screwed her foot into the sand. "Pamela?"

Pointing back towards the rock pools, Tom gestured towards a figure bent over the water. "She's a member of the family I'm staying with. Pamela's the one who showed me where the crabs hide. You'll like her, Lils."

Sam's mother would have called Pamela Groves 'a stocky girl'. Although a floral dress was wrapped around her solid frame, she looked far more at ease in the large pair of boots that encased her feet. The ragged cut of her hair suggested that she trimmed it herself. Smudges of sand decorated her face and arms, and Sam could tell that she wasn't the kind of girl who avoided hard work.

"'Ey up!" She greeted them with a wide smile and friendly, brown eyes. Sam watched the girl delve into a deep rock pool with her fishing net. The water was as clear as glass.

"Are you gonna stand there gawpin'," Pamela asked, "or do summat wi' that net o' yours?"

Tom leaned close to his two school friends. "You'll get used to her – she doesn't mean to be rude. Her mum calls it *straight talkin'*."

"Aye," Pamela nodded as her strong arms thrust her net even deeper into the water. "And you'll be straight *walkin'* back 'ome with no supper if you don't give me a hand."

Lily was the first to step forwards, brandishing her own pole net like an eager soldier. "What do you want me to do?"

"You can make yourself more useful than them two lummoxes," she said and pointed towards the largest rock in the pool. "I've been tryin' to coax out a massive crab for t' last twenty minutes. It's stubborn as 'eck but if we nab it, it'll make a crackin' meal."

Sam saw a curious crease stretch across his cousin's brow, telling Pamela that Lily was struggling to decode her words. When Pamela glanced towards him, Sam sent a similar shrug to confirm that he was struggling, too.

Pamela sighed. "Just jam that net under t' rock and gi' it a firm shuffle. If we're in luck, the beast'll run straight into me net."

Having managed to decipher most of Pamela's sentence, Lily gently eased her net into the water and steered it towards the lip of the rock. She had to move to the very edge of the water and as she strained to guide her net towards the bottom of the pool, the cold seawater began to caress her toes.

Pamela encouraged her. "Just a bit farther... that's grand. Now, jam it left, real 'ard!"

Suddenly, the salty rock pool clouded with sand and bubbles. It happened so quickly that Lily jumped back in shock, slipping on one of the rocks. Though unhurt, she was clearly disappointed to see that at the end of her dripping pole was an empty net.

None of her companions seemed to notice or care. They were all too busy staring down at the writhing contents of Pamela's net.

"It's a funny-looking crab," Sam observed.

"That thing's like a rock on stilts," Tom leaned away, as though the creature might contaminate his air. "I think you should put it back. It's giving me the creeps."

"Rubbish," Pamela insisted, holding her net aloft like a trophy. Crusty, red legs jabbed and jerked through the holes. "It's a spider crab. Those legs are filled wi' meat. This thing'll feed the 'ole family tomorrow, an' we'll still have leftovers for crab soup."

The Yorkshire girl grinned across at Sam. "There might be another in there. Get the net in there an' wiggle it around."

Sam wasn't listening. Something unusual had caught his attention in the dwindling light on the clifftop above them. His eyes darted left and right, trying to catch a second glimpse. "Someone's up there," he told the others. "Look!"

His friends followed his pointing finger as it

guided their gaze to a grassy mound on the clifftop. Their eyes were fixed on the shadowy spot when a burst of orange flashes sparked like flames.

"Looks like someone's got a torch," Pamela said.

The quartet watched in silence as more orange flashes continued – some short, others long. It seemed to go on for several minutes.

Sam and Tom glanced out to sea. The waves had grown choppier as the tide rolled its watery carpet up the beach. Sam thought that he might have briefly spotted a similar burst of flashes but when he tried to focus his gaze on its source, he saw only the rolling swell of more waves.

"Why would someone flash a torch from the top of the cliff?" Tom wondered, turning back to the clifftop. "There's only us here to see it."

"Dunno," said Sam, "but that's not normal behaviour."

"Maybe someone's stuck and needs help," Lily suggested.

"Haven't they got a pair o' lungs?" Pamela asked. "Better to shout for 'elp than flash some silly torch. More likely they're up to no good."

Tom shrugged and wrinkled his nose. "Like what?"

Sam anchored the end of his fishing net deep into the sand, then brushed a handful of fingers through his copper-coloured hair as he stepped towards the cliff. "I guess there's only one way we'll find out."

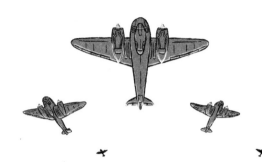

Chapter Twelve
Clues on the Clifftop

Without the benefit of Pamela's shortcut, the three Londoners would have needed over an hour to ascend Filey's crumbling cliff face. Luckily, following a zigzagging pathway known only to the locals meant that they reached the summit in under ten minutes.

Despite this, when they arrived, the clifftop was empty.

"We're too late," Sam grumbled. "They've gone."

"'Old your 'orses," Pamela said, taking charge. "Me dad was a police officer before 'e signed up to t' army. He always said people leave clues everywhere without even knowin'."

The three southern school friends were still trying to catch their breath after such a long climb as Pamela led them along the clifftop's grassy fringe. The sun was threatening to dip beneath the blunted green peaks of the Wolds, and what daylight there was now came with a chilled lick.

"How do you know where to look?" Lily asked, panting as she tried to keep up.

"Yeah," Sam agreed. "Those flashes of light could have been coming from anywhere."

Pamela launched a chuckle over her shoulder. "I've lived 'ere all me life. This cliff is like me back garden. I know exactly where to look."

She was right. In seconds, all four children were gathered around a nest of freshly crushed grass. Despite the fading light, they could clearly see the outline of whoever had been stretched out in the grass. The toes of a pair of shoes had even made a couple of ruts in the soft earth.

Pamela pointed at two similar indentations in the earth near the cliff edge. "Elbow marks, I reckon." She crouched down to get a closer look. "Someone was propped up right here – probably holding that torch like a camera."

Tom peered out across the sea again. He could see nothing. "But why? I don't understand."

"I'm more interested in who was up here," Sam said. "That's what we really need to figure out."

As the two boys scratched their heads and pondered their questions, Lily spotted something half hidden in the grass nearby. Quickly dropping to her knees, she gently peeled back the broken stalks until something familiar was revealed. She plucked the small black and red box up off the ground.

"See?" Pamela cheered. "Me dad was right. That's got to be a clue."

Lily nodded back as she waved the empty packet of Double Ace cigarettes. "It's more than a clue! I know exactly who these belong to."

"How can you be so sure?" Pamela asked. "Lots of people smoke those things."

"My mum says they're disgusting," Tom said, screwing up his face. "I reckon it must taste like you're chewing chimney soot."

"Our neighbour, Missus Patterson, says they're good for her," Sam remembered. "She reckons the tobacco smoke cleanses her lungs."

"Sounds like it's poached her brain," Tom argued. "How can breathing smoke be good for you? My mum reckons that years from now, doctors will tell us that smoking cigarettes makes us ill."

"Pah," Sam snorted. "There's more chance of someone flying to the moon and back."

Lily ignored the boys' bickering and passed the Double Ace box to Pamela.

"Missus Scales smokes the same brand, so she writes her name on the back of the packet. That way, she knows which ones are hers."

Pamela studied the little box. When she looked across at Lily, she seemed confused. "But there's no name on 'ere."

Lily shook her head confidently. "That's because these don't belong to her. They belong to her lodger."

Sam felt his stomach lurch. Even though his feelings about the lodger had recently taken a turn towards suspicion, he didn't feel that this was sound enough proof that Albert had been here.

"How can you be sure?" asked Tom quizzically.

"I bet loads of people in town smoke these."

Pamela nodded. "Aye, an' any one of 'em could have been up 'ere."

As the others continued to debate over the owner of the cigarette packet, Tom began to study the ground once more. Suddenly he cried out. "Hey, what's this?" He reached down and plucked something from the grass and brought it over to the group. Held between his index finger and thumb was a gold ring.

"Another clue!" Pamela held out her palm and Tom carefully placed the ring into her outstretched hand. All four children leaned in for a closer look.

"Maybe whoever was here dropped this as well," Tom suggested. "It's large... looks like a man's ring, don't you reckon?"

Sam glanced at Lily. He knew what she was thinking.

"Well, did you 'appen to notice whether this lodger was wearin' a ring?" Pamela turned her attention to Lily.

"I'm not sure... I... yeah, maybe," Lily stuttered. "Yes, now I'm thinking about it. Sam, you believe me, don't you?" she pleaded.

Sam frowned. "I dunno, Lils... I don't like him either, but we can't be sure that he was up here."

"It was him," Lily insisted, turning from each unconvinced face to the next. "I just *know*."

*

Lily gripped Sam's arm tightly as they both walked up the track towards the unwelcoming farmhouse. They'd managed to hitch a ride into Muston on another RAF truck and, even though dusk was threatening to suck the light from the darkening blue sky, Lily hoped that her hosts would forgive her lateness.

Sam's mind was on other things. The children had all decided that it was best if Sam kept the gold ring for now, until they could be certain where it had come from. Lily didn't dare take it back to the Scales' farm and Pamela had said her mother was, in her own words, 'a nosy parker'. So, Sam had stuck it in his trouser pocket for safekeeping. He thought back to his encounter with the tall, dark-haired man who had been so aggressive with him earlier that day. "So, this Albert bloke," he said, keeping his voice light and airy, "what makes you think that he's so bad?"

Lily shrugged. "I dunno. I don't like him, though. I told you before – he gives me the creeps."

"Why isn't he in the army, like our dads?" Sam wondered out loud.

"Maybe he's a vicar," suggested Lily. "They don't have to go to war."

This was true. Sam knew that some of his schoolmates had fathers who had stayed in their jobs at home, rather than being conscripted. Medical workers, prison officers and those with health problems were often excused from service, as well as coal miners, shipbuilders and anyone else whose job helped the war effort.

"Oh, aye?" sneered an unpleasant voice from

behind them. "An' what would a couple o' bone 'eads like you two know about that?"

Sam and Lily turned to find themselves face to face with two lumbering teenagers. Lily gripped her cousin's arm even tighter and Sam felt her begin to tremble. He recognised the voice from the woods: the pair had to be Vincent and Duncan Scales.

In the day's fading light, the two boys could easily have passed for trolls. They were certainly big enough. Twisted teeth sat behind thick, cracked lips and hair cut to the scalp made both boys' ears jut out like trophy handles.

The largest of the two brothers glared at Sam through narrowed eyes. "Eh, Dunc, who've we got 'ere?" Vincent prodded Sam's shoulder with a thick, calloused finger. The blow made Sam wince.

"Looks like another one o' them 'omeless scroungers from London," the smaller of the two brothers said. Duncan was still tall enough to tower over Sam and his two clenched fists suggested that he was every bit as mean as his older brother.

The two boys walked around Sam and Lily in a slow, deliberate circle. Fingers as hard as sticks jabbed and prodded Sam from every angle. He felt trapped.

"Leave us alone," Sam ordered. "We've done nothing wrong."

Vincent cackled hoarsely. "Did you 'ear that, Dunc? They've done nothin' wrong!"

Duncan stopped prowling and stepped close to Sam. His unfriendly grin revealed several gaps in the top row of his crooked teeth. The smell of his sweat and stale breath made Sam turn away.

"You've come up from fancy London to eat our food an' sleep under our roofs," the largest boy growled. "An' now, you're trespassing on our land."

"We're not trespassing," Sam argued. "Lily lives here."

"We're not talkin' about this silly mare," Duncan said. He glared briefly at Lily before turning his attention back towards Sam. "I'm talkin' about you. Didn't you see that sign on t' gate?"

Sam remembered noticing the hand-painted board which told trespassers to *Keep Out.*

"Happen they don't teach these evacuees to read," Vincent cackled again. "Happen they're all as stupid as each other."

Lily yelped as the smaller brother suddenly wrestled her free from Sam's arm. When instinct launched Sam's arms towards her, Duncan stepped between them both, slamming an elbow into Sam's chest.

Sam fell back onto the ground, winded and in pain. Lily objected noisily until one of Vincent's muddy hands clamped itself across her mouth.

"Take 'er up to t' house," Duncan told his brother. "Our ma'll sort 'er out. Leave me to deal wi' this filthy trespasser."

Still nursing his throbbing chest and gasping to

catch his breath, Sam was powerless to resist as Duncan dragged him up off the ground. Hands and arms made strong through years of working the land lifted Sam as though he were nothing more than a scarecrow.

"We don't want t' likes of you round 'ere," the teenager hissed.

Over his assailant's shoulder, Sam could see Lily being dragged towards the farm. She seemed as helpless as he was.

"Leave her alone!" Sam ordered. "Don't you dare hurt her!"

There was a pitch to Duncan's laugh that sounded cold and sharp. "It's not 'er you should be worryin' about."

Sam felt a chill race down his spine as the Scales boy tightened his grip. Strong fingers held him like a vice.

"That sign on t' gate is there for a reason," Duncan continued. "P'raps you'll give it more heed after I've taught you a lesson."

Fighting his pain, Sam summoned as much strength as he could muster in a struggle to wriggle free, but Duncan's grip was too powerful. There was nothing that Sam could do, nor was there any way that he could avoid the clubbing right fist that swung through the air towards him.

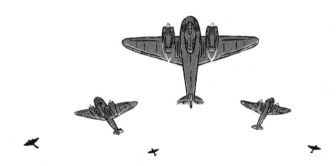

Chapter Thirteen
Detectives in the Dark

"Blimey, Sam. What happened to your eye?" asked Tom Mahoney.

Pamela peered at Sam's wound with concern, sucking a sharp blast of air between her teeth.

Sam had answered the knock on the door and was pleased to find the two familiar faces greeting him at the doorstep. He grabbed his jacket from a wobbly wall hook and slipped out of the cottage.

"It's nothing," he lied as he bustled Tom and Pamela back down the garden path. "I fell and hit my face on a tree, that's all."

It was already late in the afternoon and Sam was relieved to have an excuse to get out of the house. Mrs Ward had spent a large part of the day bombarding him with awkward questions about his bruised eye. It hadn't seemed to matter that she had already grilled him about his injury for over thirty minutes the previous evening.

As the trio walked towards Filey centre, Tom stared at the grazed and swollen flesh around his friend's eye.

"That's odd," Pamela said. "I 'eard one o' those Scales boys boastin' about giving a good 'idin' to a trespasser 'e caught up at t' farm last night."

Sam stayed silent.

"Says it was one of us London lads," Tom continued. "Says he gave him a black eye. Couldn't be you though Sam, eh? 'Cause your eye's purple."

Feeling embarrassed, Sam quickly changed the subject "I've been thinking about that light we saw from the clifftop."

"You mean the cigarette lighter?" Tom asked.

"Who said it was a cigarette lighter?"

"I did," Pamela told him. "We were talkin' yesterday. At first, we thought it was odd. But then we realised it was likely just someone lightin' their Double Ace."

Sam's sore eye throbbed as his brow creased. "How many cigarettes do you think he was smoking?"

Tom dismissed the question. "If his lighter fuel was running out, he'd have to keep trying. That's why it was flashing so much. Pamela's really smart, you know. She's top of her class at school, and her dad was..."

"Yeah, yeah," Sam interrupted. "A police officer. I remember."

"It makes sense," Pamela insisted. "I mean, what other explanation is there?"

Although Sam couldn't think of one there and then, he still wasn't convinced. As far as he could remember, the flashes had been far too frequent to come from someone trying to light a cigarette – any smoker would have given up long before the flashes had ceased. Besides, there had been something about the pattern of flashes that had seemed far too deliberate.

Having spent most of his day behind the closed door of his bedroom, Sam had already had plenty of time to dwell on yesterday's events – and when he hadn't been thinking about ways to get revenge on the Scales brothers, he had been replaying those flashing clifftop lights in his mind. The more he'd thought about it, the more he'd found himself arriving at the same unsettling conclusion.

"I think there might be something fishy going on," he told his companions.

Pamela sniffed the air and then sniggered. "Ah, that'll be t' trawlers landing their catches in Scarborough."

Sam was too focused to share the joke. "I don't think it's a coincidence that we found an empty packet of cigarettes on the cliff."

"D'you think they really belong to Lily's lodger friend?" Tom asked.

Pamela shook her head vigorously. "I asked me mam what she knew about 'im last night," she said confidently. "She reckons 'e's really quiet, helps out at the church an' never gives anyone any trouble."

Sam replied, "I'm not sure. He scares Lily to death and when we followed him through the backstreets, he wasn't happy."

Pamela gasped. "You followed him?"

Tom's eyes widened. "Where did he go?"

"He cornered me in an alley next to a barber's shop," Sam told them. "He was really angry that I'd been following him. I thought he was going to give me a real hiding."

"I'm not surprised! Did 'e did that to your eye?" asked Pamela.

"No, no, this happened later. When I, uh..."

"Fell into a tree?" Tom reminded him.

Ignoring him, Sam continued. "Anyway, it's possible that he could have been heading for the clifftop –"

"But why?" Pamela wondered. "There's nowt but grass an' seagulls on t' cliff. What's the big secret?"

"I dunno," Sam admitted. "But I think we should go back there later and find out. If he's there again, we might be able to figure out what he's up to."

*

It wasn't quite nightfall. The sky above the trio's heads was the colour of rusting iron, as the last lick of the day's sunlight swept its orange tongue from east to west. Yet, as Sam peered over the lip of the large rock they were hiding behind, a brightly glowing full moon told him that a curtain the colour of oil would soon reach across the entire sky.

Around them, dark shadows loomed from the

base of rock clusters, filling the beach's carpet of sand with what resembled an army of ogres. At their backs, the distant growl of restless waves told him that the tide was still in retreat. Pamela had promised that it would be several hours before it reached their vantage point in the shadows of the great Brigg. It was certainly comforting to know that they wouldn't suddenly be swept out to sea. It also allowed them to be patient – well, two of them, at least.

"This is boring," Tom complained, "and it's cold."

"Cold?" Pamela spluttered. "This is nowt. Wait till I bring you down 'ere in t' winter. Them North Sea gales can soon turn your blood to ice." She gave Sam's ribs a playful nudge. "Me old grandad got frostbite fishin' for scallops in these rock pools, three winters past."

"I know how he feels," Tom grumbled, rubbing his hands together in an attempt to keep his fingers warm. "How much longer are we going to wait down here?"

Sam didn't have a watch but the sun's slow slide towards the horizon had probably taken an hour, maybe longer. So far, there had been no flashes from the clifftop. Even Sam was beginning to wonder if they were wasting their time.

"Maybe 'e *was* just lighting his cigarettes," Pamela wondered. "Me mam says that for some folks, lookin' out to sea is really relaxin'."

"Yeah, but your mum also says that eating sprouts will make me grow up big and strong," Tom grumbled. "Yet all they do is give me wretched wind."

Pamela waved her hand beneath her nose, grinning. "Aye, an' don't we all know it!"

"Shurrup!"

"Shh!" Sam interrupted the duo's bickering. "I think I saw something!"

All three sets of eyes locked onto the clifftop as they held their collective breath. Moments later, they gasped in unison.

"I saw it," Tom said, pointing to a spot close to

where they'd discovered the discarded Double Ace packet and ring the previous evening.

"Me too," Pamela agreed. "Look – another one."

All three children watched as more flashes pierced the gloom like pistol sparks.

"He's not lighting cigarettes tonight," Tom observed.

Pamela agreed. "Nah! That definitely looks like some kind o' signal to me. But who the 'eck's he signalling to in t' middle of t' sea?"

Together, the trio spun round to gaze out across the distant waves. At first, they saw nothing but the undulating swirl of the ocean. Then, from a spot close to where the arm of Filey Brigg gave way to the sea, pinpricks of yellow light suddenly began to flash a now-familiar pattern.

"Blimey!" Pamela yelped. "There's something out there."

"Maybe it's a fishing boat," Tom wondered.

"Oh, right? And what's Albert doin'? Sendin' Missus Scales' order for fresh fish 'n' chips?"

"OK, smarty-pants," Tom bristled. "Why don't *you* tell us what he's doing, then?"

"I've got a better idea," Sam said. "Why don't we write the flashes down?"

"Why?" asked Pamela.

"How?" Tom added.

Taking charge, Sam nodded at Tom before pointing towards the sand. "Some flashes last longer than others. I'll tell you them as I see them, and you can write them in the sand."

"How do I write flashes?"

"I dunno. Just improvise," said Sam. "I'll let you know when the light starts and stops." He turned to Pamela. "You shout the same thing for our flashes, and I'll keep watching out to sea."

"I still don't understand," Pamela admitted. "Why does it matter if the flashes are long or short?"

"I don't know, either," Sam replied. "But we can work that out later."

*

"Slow down, Sam," Tom urged. "I can't keep up!"

He was crouched above the sand, scratching a series of lines into the damp surface. The pattern that he had sketched so far looked like something from the wall of an Egyptian pyramid. It made no sense at all.

"It's not me," Sam explained. "It's the flashes."

At first, Sam had tried to signal to Tom every time that the light had turned on and off. However, after Tom had complained that he kept losing track, Sam had adopted a much simpler method.

"Oh no, there's more: short... short... long... short. Pause. Long... long... long... Pause. Short... long... short..."

Tom frantically gouged more marks into the sand, then squealed in frustration as Pamela began to bark out instructions of her own.

When the flashes finally ceased, Tom was breathless and weary. As his two friends hauled him to his feet, all three of them gazed down at the lines etched across the beach.

"This is gibberish," Tom panted. "It makes no sense at all."

"Maybe not to us," Sam agreed, "but it must mean something to somebody."

"It definitely looks like some kind o' code to me," Pamela told them. She took a step back from Tom's handiwork. "This is dangerous stuff, I reckon."

"Dangerous?" Tom scoffed. "It's just harmless scribbles in the sand."

"Aye, it is to us," Pamela warned. "But it's what that lot means that worries me. What if it's top-secret stuff? You know, war stuff. Or worse!"

"What's worse than war stuff?" Tom whispered.

They all stayed silent for a moment, pondering Pamela's warning. Finally, Tom broke the silence. "I'll wipe it clean," he volunteered, moving towards his sandy hieroglyphics.

"No!" Sam seized his friend's arm, dragging him clear of the lines, some of which were vertical, to show short flashes, and some horizontal, to show long ones. "Not yet."

Tom tugged himself free. Moonlight shone onto his face, revealing a scowl of confusion. "Why? Some things are better unknown. I don't want to get into any trouble. It's bad enough that we've been sent away, Sam. This kind of stuff should be left to grown-ups."

"Maybe," Sam said, placing himself between his friend and the code, "but we can't just ignore this."

"Sam's right," Pamela agreed, landing a placatory hand onto Tom's shoulder. "We need to tell someone about this."

Shrugging Pamela's hand away, Tom asked, "Tell someone what? That we've drawn a load of lines in the sand? By the time we get back into the town and convince someone to come down here, the sea will have washed it all away. We'll end up looking like a bunch of idiots."

"We can write it down," Sam suggested. He looked towards the sea which had now begun its slow crawl back up the beach. "We still have time."

"Maybe," Tom shrugged. "But we don't have a pencil or any paper. And we're not likely to find any out here, are we?"

"You don't need a pencil or paper," Pamela

assured them. "Wait here."

The two boys watched silently as Pamela raced to the foot of the Brigg. There, she knelt in the darkness and began to rummage through the carpet of sea-smoothed rocks and stones.

"Most of the time, I have no idea what she's doing," Tom said quietly. "It's like I'm living with an alien."

"Life's different up here," Sam replied. The clank and clatter of stones being discarded mixed with the growing rumble of approaching waves. "They have their own way of doing things, and so do we. I guess we just have to adapt."

Finally, Pamela jumped to her feet and followed her own tracks in the sand back to the boys.

"Here!" She handed each of them two rocks. One was as round as a dinner plate, and almost as white. The other was much smaller and dark.

"What are we supposed to do with these?" Tom asked. "Play some kind of strange northern sport?"

"Blimey, don't you two know owt?" Pamela snatched the stones from Tom's hands and stepped towards the lines of code. "Look!"

Using the small, dark stone, she slowly began to scratch lines across the surface of the larger white stone.

"The small stone is coal, washed up from t' sea bed," she told them both. "This white rock is chalk, from t' cliffs down the coast at Flamborough. If you press t' coal hard enough, you can leave a mark on t' chalk."

She handed the stones back to Tom, then retreated back to the pebble carpet to find her own. After exchanging embarrassed glances, the two boys silently began to fill their chalk plates with coal marks. As they worked, it soon became obvious that they were going to need more stones.

Chapter Fourteen
Code-Cracking for Beginners

Sam woke the next day with a sense of purpose that he hadn't felt since the onset of Hitler's bombing raids. As he enjoyed the caress of his soft pillow and blinked away sleepiness to an orchestra of birdsong from the tree branches outside, he knew that he had something purposeful to do. He had a mission.

Aided by his friends, he had managed to copy most of Tom's sand scribbles onto six large chalk stones. The trio had then carried them from the beach to Mrs Ward's house, stowing them in a dry alcove between the shed and the house, safely out of reach of any night-time rain showers.

Having bounced out of bed and dressed quickly, Sam skipped his morning wash in favour of getting straight to work. He'd promised Tom and Pamela that he would transfer their coal etchings onto paper as soon as he got up, then meet them outside Filey's town library at lunchtime.

Unfortunately, he'd slept later than he'd hoped and the brass carriage clock sitting on Mrs Ward's mantelpiece told him that it was already well past ten. Urgency quickened his step, propelling him into the kitchen where shock stopped him in his tracks like a solid wall.

"Missus Ward, what are you doing?!" he shrieked.

His host looked up from the table and smiled a warm greeting. "Good mornin' to you too, Sam."

Sam shook his head in disbelief as his eyes gazed down at the contents of the kitchen table. Instead of the usual mix of condiment pots and cork placemats, the table was decorated with six large, white chalk stones.

"Where... where did you get those?" he babbled.

"You know where I got 'em, Sam," Mrs Ward cheerfully replied. "I know you probably meant to surprise me with 'em, but I found 'em next to t' shed and couldn't resist getting to work on 'em straight away."

He could feel panic beginning to constrict his throat. "Getting to work?"

Nodding, Mrs Ward pointed to the bowl of soapy water resting beside her elbow. "Someone's scrawled all over 'em, so I thought I'd scrub 'em clean before I add 'em to me rock garden. They'll make a beautiful feature!"

Mrs Ward had clearly been busy; four of the stones had been scrubbed so clean that all traces of the black lines had now completely vanished. In fact, they'd been cleaned so thoroughly that the surface of the scrubbed chalk was even brighter than freshly fallen snow.

A fifth stone was resting on the table in front of Mrs Ward. Half of its surface had already been rubbed clean and what marks remained were smudged and barely readable. Only one of the stones remained untouched.

Almost numbed by distress, Sam half walked, half staggered towards the table. Mrs Ward reached out to steady him. "Sam, are you alright?"

"Yeah, yeah," he lied, frantically trying to clear his head and come up with a new plan. He didn't feel that he could tell anyone about the flashes of light yet, not even Mrs Ward – at least, not until he'd figured out what they meant.

"I just wanted to surprise you with these, that's all," he lied. "I wanted to clean them myself."

"Ah, you're such a kind-spirited lad." Mrs Ward reached up and ruffled his hair with her damp fingers. She then slid the remaining stone towards him. "'Ere, you can 'elp wi' this one, if you like."

Sam snatched the stone off the table and said, "I'll... uh... I'll just get some... uh... some fresh water And a cloth from... from the shed." He began to back out of the kitchen, cradling the stone against his chest as though it were made of solid gold.

"Good idea," said Mrs Ward and, to Sam's surprise, she stood up. "But you stay here, there's dangerous stuff in that shed. I'll get you my 'enry's wire brush," she added. "These black marks take some shiftin'."

*

"Missus Ward did *what*?!" Disbelief transformed Tom's question into a cry.

"She cleaned them," Sam told him again as he leaned against the frame of the town library's doorway. "With soap and a cloth. She thought they were for the garden."

"Why didn't you stop 'er?" Pamela asked. Both hands were clamped to her cheeks in horror.

"I was asleep," Sam explained. "By the time I'd got up and ready, there was only one stone left. I had to copy it quickly while she was out of the room and then I had to scrub it before I could give it back."

They all stared down at the scrap of paper in Sam's palm. It didn't look like very much, now. All three sets of eyes lingered on the now-familiar pattern of lines.

Eventually, Pamela clapped her hands together and tried to chase away their disappointment. "Well, at least you managed to rescue one of 'em. An' I reckon decoding this should be easier than trying to tackle all six, eh?"

The two boys nodded weakly.

"It took ages to write that all down," Tom grumbled.

"Yeah, and what if the most important bits have been scrubbed clean?" Sam added.

"There's nowt we can do about that now, is there?" Pamela pointed out. "An' like me old grandad always said, there's no point cryin' over spilt beer."

"Milk!" Tom said.

"Eh?"

"It's spilt milk," Tom insisted. "There's no point crying over spilt milk."

Pamela shook her head. "Not in me grandad's house, it ain't!"

All three children laughed, glad to finally find something to distract them from their disappointments. They were still chuckling as Sam pushed open the library door and led his friends into the warmth of the building.

*

The library was as quiet as a church. Two middle-aged ladies busied themselves with the task of stacking books onto shelves as Sam settled himself at a table. A stack of hardbound volumes teetered by one elbow. Pamela and Tom sat on chairs opposite him. Smaller piles were perched in front of them.

"So, what are we looking for?" Tom asked, eyeing his pile of books with clear suspicion. "Books always remind me of school."

"What's wrong wi' school?" Pamela snapped.

"Our teacher's great – we learn lots o' useful stuff all t' time."

Tom scratched his head, wincing as though it was hurting him to think. "Yeah, our school's all right, too. It's my brain that lets me down – it seems to want to learn at a different pace to everyone else's."

"Learning's not a competition," Sam assured him. "My Aunt Peg always says that knowledge will drop into your head when it's good and ready."

Tom shuffled in his seat. "Well, I sometimes wish it would hurry up."

The trio exchanged giggles before Sam pulled the largest book from the top of the stack. "There has to be something in one of these books that explains these markings." He dropped the heavy book onto the table in front of Tom, who opened the cover. "Remember – look for anything relating to light, or flashes." Soon, all three children were immersed in the pages of their books.

Sam's first book was of little help. Most of its chapter headings covered written codes, or secret codes hidden in numbers or language. One chapter was entirely devoted to Egyptian hieroglyphics. Nothing covered flashes of light.

Pamela was running her finger down the contents page of one of the other books. "You know, me old dad says that t' Germans 'ave been using their own secret code for years. He's 'eard that we've got whole teams o' boffins working down in some secret location, an' all they do all day is try to decode intercepted messages."

"All day?" Sam grumbled. "I'm surprised they can stay awake."

After reading almost an entire chapter on semaphore, then realising that the flag-waving code couldn't possibly be replicated by flashes of light, Sam was beginning to give up hope.

"It's not often we see readers as young as you in 'ere," one of the librarians said. She was pushing a trolley loaded with books and eyed Sam's stack with interest. She picked up one of his discarded volumes and read the title. "You three are a little young to be joinin' the signal corps, aren't you?"

Sam gazed up at her, puzzled.

The lady grinned. "Isn't that why you're studyin' codes? Fancy 'avin a go at crackin' those Jerry messages, do you?"

"Oh, no," Sam shook his head. He didn't want to tell her about the clifftop lights. "I... uh... my friend has sent me a message in code. If I can figure out what it says, she'll let me have her sweet rations."

The librarian seemed far more interested in the pages of Sam's books. "Me 'usband Jim were a radio operator in t' Great War. He used to send messages from t' trenches to t' command post. Says there ain't a code invented that he couldn't understand." She leaned close. "He'd be no good as a spy, though – he told me all his secrets."

Tom glanced up from the pages of his book. Hope swam in his eyes. "So, do you know about codes, too?"

The librarian nodded. "Mostly Morse code."

"What's that?"

"Dots and dashes," the lady explained. "With gaps between. Each letter of t' alphabet 'as its own unique pattern."

"Dots and dashes?" Tom repeated, looking unimpressed.

The librarian continued. "It's usually transmitted by radio. T' operator taps out a message usin' a special device." As she rapped her finger against the tabletop, drumming out a pattern of light and heavy beats, Sam felt his hopes fade. "But if he doesn't have a radio, the same message can be sent using a signal lamp, or a torch. Even a mirror reflecting sunlight would do the trick. Short and long flashes can be read in the same way."

Sam could feel excitement bubbling in his stomach as he glanced down at the markings on the scrap of paper. Tom had been so close with his lines, but the vertical ones needed changing to dots instead. "Do you have a book about it?" he asked quickly.

"No," the lady replied, "but your friend does." She plucked one of Tom's discarded publications off the desk and passed it to Sam, who ran his finger over gold-leaf lettering which read *Code-Cracking for Beginners*. "There should be an entire chapter about Morse code in 'ere."

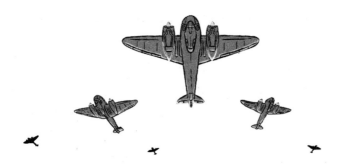

Chapter Fifteen
Stealing Wheels from Soldiers

"I've been staring at these marks for so long, my poor eyes think they've got measles," Tom grumbled.

"We need to check them again," Pamela insisted, staring down at the scrap of paper that Sam had scribbled on. It contained a translation of Tom's lines into neat dots and dashes. Sitting beneath each separate pattern was also a letter of the alphabet.

"We've decoded it three times, now," Tom reminded her, "and each time, it says the same thing. What's the point in checking again?"

"Tom's right," Sam nodded.

As the helpful librarian had promised, the book contained an entire chapter on Morse code. The three children had huddled together, eagerly poring through the pages until they had reached the most important section: a decoding sheet.

Armed with that, they had been able to make sense of the white rock's etchings, but it had been slow work. Both Tom and Pamela had wanted to be the one to decode the messages, each checking then double-checking the other's work. In the end, it had been Sam who had decoded the final few lines of code. Now, they all stared down at his scribbles, not quite wanting the words to be correct.

"It's pointless doing it all again," he insisted. "We'd just come up with the same sentence and we'd be wasting valuable time."

"But what if we've got it wrong?" Pamela jabbed her finger towards Sam's paper. "It's words like this that can get folk into trouble. Words like this will get *us* into trouble, especially if they're wrong! We can't go accusing anyone of this sort of thing –"

Sam snatched the scrap of paper up off the desk and folded it into his pocket. As he leapt to his feet, he said, "I don't care. I'd rather be wrong and get into trouble than not tell somebody what the code says. If we say nothing and this turns out to be true, how will we feel?"

His two friends replied with a slow and reluctant nod. Pamela folded her arms across her chest and snorted like an irritated sow. "So, what are we gonna do?"

Sam was still trying to figure out an answer when the friendly librarian passed by again. He snatched her sleeve. "Excuse me – who's in charge around here?"

His reply was a puzzled stare. "In t' library?"

"No, in Filey," Sam snapped. "Who runs the town?"

Creases around the librarian's eyes made Sam wonder if his tone had offended her. He wanted to apologise but didn't have time.

The woman shrugged. "It used to be t' mayor, I

suppose. But now, I'm not so sure. It seems like those fly-boys up at Mister Butlin's place tell everyone what to do these days."

Sam danced from foot to foot, fighting an itch that urged him to get moving. "And who's in charge there?"

"The bloke wi' t' biggest hat, I reckon. But they'll never speak to you," she snorted. "They're far too busy."

As the librarian returned to her book-stacking, Pamela wrapped strong fingers around Sam's forearm. "She's right, Sam. You'll never get them soldiers to listen to you. If me dad wasn't in t' army, we could tell 'im."

Sam didn't share his friend's despondency. He knew that there was at least one soldier who might listen to him. "Let me worry about that," he told her. "I've got to at least try to warn them."

"Sam's right," Tom agreed, turning to Pamela. "And we've got to help him."

"No!" Sam barked. Although the message they had decoded carried a frightening warning, it was the hidden danger it also contained that worried Sam just as much.

"Albert is still at the farmhouse," he reminded his friends. "If Lily's right and he's involved with this, it makes him a very dangerous man –"

Tom suddenly gasped, as if he'd been struck in the guts by a heavy blow. "Lily is there, too." His eyes bulged like eggs. "If she's right, she could be in danger."

Sam had been fighting the urge to run straight to the farm at Muston since the moment they had decoded the last words. He nodded at his friends. "That's why I want you to go straight there. Look after Lily until I get there with the soldiers. Don't let anything bad happen to her."

*

The tall sentry who stood guard at the gate of RAF Hunmanby peered down at Sam as though he were a stray dog. The barrel of the soldier's rifle seemed to make a target of his chest.

"This is no place for a kid," he barked. "Make yourself scarce, unless you want a matching black eye."

Sam ignored the warning. "I need to speak to Corporal Timmins."

The guard stepped forward, looming over him. "What you need to do is clear off!"

Despite the intimidation, Sam held his ground. "He told me to come here. He knows me. Ask him yourself. This is *important*!"

The guard used the end of his rifle to herd Sam away from the camp gate. "We're not here to babysit local kids. There's a war on, remember? That's what's important. Now, get lost!"

Sam ducked as the guard aimed a swinging palm towards his ear. A drumbeat of anger and frustration thumped behind his rib cage. He'd never felt so powerless.

"You don't *understand*!" Sam seethed. "We're in danger. You're in danger. Something bad is going to happen."

The guard smirked unkindly. "Don't tell me – sweet rations are going to be halved? Or is your bedtime going to be even earlier?" The humour vanished from the guard's face as he snarled down at Sam. "Run along and play hide-and-seek."

Sam backed away, glaring towards the camp. At any other time, the soldier's dismissive words might have annoyed him, but he'd always known that trying to contact Corporal Timmins had been a long shot. Grown-ups rarely listened to children; since war had broken out, most of the adults that he knew had become absorbed by their own worries and fear.

If he was going to do anything about the secret that he'd learned at the library, he was going to need more proof. One cigarette packet and a gold ring weren't enough to start pointing fingers. That meant returning to Scales Farm, where he and Lily could find out more about the lodger – Lily's hunch wasn't much to go on, but it was a start. That also meant getting to the village of Muston fast, and Sam couldn't do that on two feet.

Luckily, fortune stepped in. There, propped against one of the green dormitory blocks which ran parallel to the RAF base's ten-foot perimeter fence, was something that could take him to Lily's front door in a matter of minutes: a green RAF-issue bicycle!

The guard's gaze tracked Sam as he retraced his steps, following the road that ran beside the fence and back towards Filey. When the driver of a returning truck stole the soldier's attention, Sam seized his opportunity. He quickly pulled himself up onto the fence and used the skills that he had honed by clambering over London's warehouse fences to haul himself into the camp.

Not caring whether he'd been spotted or not, he sprinted across a stretch of grass that looked like it might have been used as a football pitch. Sam reached the first line of green dormitory huts in less than a minute. The absence of yells and cries told him that his invasion had so far gone unnoticed.

Realising that his good fortune wouldn't last forever, he zigzagged through the gaps between buildings until he found himself crouching beside the rubber wheels of the bicycle. The guard was still busy talking to the driver of the vehicle, so Sam climbed up onto the bicycle's saddle and began to pedal for all he was worth.

By the time both tyres had skidded onto the thin road which led out of the camp, the bicycle was travelling at the speed of a galloping horse.

"Hey!" cried a startled pilot as Sam narrowly avoided him. "What are you doing?"

Two more soldiers dived noisily out of the way as Sam pedalled furiously towards the exit. Their yelps brought a worried response from

the tall guard. Fortunately, by the time that he had identified the rapidly approaching rider, it was too late. Sam whizzed by him like a record-chasing racer and blew a huge raspberry into the befuddled man's face as he passed.

"Tell Corporal Timmins I've borrowed the bicycle," he cheered. "I'll be at Scales Farm if he wants it back!"

Chapter Sixteen
Propelling Pine Cones

Although the track leading from Muston Lane to the farmhouse was empty, Sam knew better than to think he could ride up it unnoticed. The windows of the old stone house faced down onto the dusty road like a sentinel's gaze, and he felt certain that at least one pair of curious eyes would see his approach.

The farm itself looked as unfriendly as its occupants. The old house might once have been painted white, but a combination of Yorkshire's harsh winters and a lack of care had created a shade of mottled grey. The barns and outbuildings on either side of the house hadn't fared much better. Some were missing part of their roofs and it looked like a succession of gales had ripped strips of wood from several walls. Although Sam couldn't see into those buildings, he was pretty sure that people could see out.

So, after concealing the bicycle beneath a mound of bracken leaves, he traversed the woodland with its thick tree trunks and made his way towards the farm unseen. He kept his wits about him, pausing every thirty seconds to make sure that his were the only feet making noises. He was pleased not to hear any telltale twig snaps or leaf rustles. So far, Sam was alone.

As he neared the farm, all that changed. Boisterous voices reached into the thatch of trees from the farmyard itself. Even before the treeline gave way to strong wooden fencing, Sam knew to whom those voices belonged. The sound of both Scales brothers was unmistakable.

Sam's fingers reached for his sore eye as he peered around a gnarly tree trunk. Despite being caught up in the urgency of reaching Lily, he had been expecting to bump into Tom and Pamela by now, perhaps hiding somewhere within the treeline as he was. They'd had a headstart on him, after all, and a wriggle of worry had already begun to make Sam wonder why he had yet to find them.

Unfortunately, he found the answer to that particular puzzle when he stared across the farm's courtyard.

As courtyards go, the rectangular channel between the back of the farmhouse and its terrace of barns and lean-tos was crude and scruffy. Pieces of unloved farm machinery sat rusting in corners like the bare bones of metal corpses. Several buckled feeding troughs slumped miserably against the farm wall and a dripping water pump fed a damp puddle which was otherwise surrounded by a desert of worn cobbles and dirt. Yet it wasn't the farm's unkempt appearance that alarmed Sam. It was the sight of Duncan and Vincent Scales accosting their latest victims.

"What is it wi' you lot from London?" Duncan growled, jabbing an iron-strong finger into the middle of Tom's chest. "Don't you know what *Keep Out* means?"

"Hey!" Pamela barked, reaching out to slap the boy's hand away. "That's assault."

"Nay, lass..." Vincent corrected her.

When Sam saw a familiar sneer curl the lips of the eldest Scales brother like the snarl of a petulant dog, he knew what was coming next.

"...this is assault!"

Vincent stiffened his wrist before slamming his thick, calloused palm into Pamela's shoulder. Her body hit the ground so hard that the loud slap launched a gang of starlings from the treetops.

"Her dad's a policeman," Tom warned the brothers. "You'll cop it for that."

"You mean 'e *was* a policeman," Duncan sneered. "But 'e went away with t' army, like the rest o' the town's do-gooders. Nowt much 'e can do from where 'e is, though, eh?"

"That's right, Dunc," Vincent agreed, nodding as he stood over Pamela. His glowering eyes seemed to dare her to move. "Times 'ave changed since Jerry gave the rest o' Europe what for. Her dad an' 'is like used to make our lives a misery before t' war began."

The boy's jigsaw of thick facial muscles creased into an even more unpleasant pattern as he began to talk in a voice that was clearly meant to be somebody else. "'Don't do this...' 'Stop going there...' 'You can't do that...'"

"Ha!" Duncan joined in. "Well, there's no one around to stop us now, is there?"

"Aye," Vincent continued. "War isn't always a bad thing."

Pamela glowered up at the brothers from the dusty courtyard floor. Even from his hiding place behind the tree trunk, Sam could sense his friend's fury.

"You two'll be locked up for talkin' like that," she scolded them both. "Me ma says that good men are givin' their lives to stop Hitler spreadin' his poison, and 'ere's you two, sounding like a couple o' turncoats."

Vincent pressed the thick sole of his boot hard against Pamela's shin, grinding it against her bone until he dragged a painful shriek from his victim.

"An' who's gonna lock me up?" he sneered. "Your dad? No, 'cause no one's 'ere, are they? Now, people like me an' our Duncan are runnin' things. We've got as much food as we want and no nosy parkers are snoopin' around us no more. If you ask me, this war can last as long as it likes."

Anger and loyalty were both urging Sam to rescue his friends. He had already scanned the forest floor for a potential weapon, finding the remains of a broken branch which would make a handy club – yet he knew that violence would get him nowhere. The brothers were too big and strong to be overpowered; Sam's bruised eye was a reminder of that.

He was desperately trying to come up with a smarter plan of action when another familiar voice sent a shiver of fear skittering down his spine.

"I thought I told you two lazy oafs to go an' catch me some rabbits for tea!" Mrs Scales bellowed from beyond the farmhouse door.

When the woman stepped out into the daylight, Sam was reminded that her two sons had inherited their troll-like features from their mother.

"If I 'ave to tell you again, I'll – oh!" The large woman froze as her gaze bounced from Tom to Pamela. A disturbing grin pulled her lips wide. "Well, well, well... no one told me we 'ad guests."

"Snoopers, more like," Duncan said, "lookin' for trouble."

Heavy footsteps carried Mrs Scales across the courtyard. "Trouble? There's no trouble 'ere. Not so long as folks keep their nosy snouts out of our business."

"We came to see our friend," Tom told her. "We just wanted to make sure she was all right."

"All right?" Mrs Scales came to a halt less than an arm's length from the children. Her unpleasant grin looked like it had been painted across her face. "An' why wouldn't that good-for-nowt creature be all right?"

"Somebody gave my friend a black eye last night." Tom jerked a finger towards one brother, then the next. "I think it was one of these."

Clearly thinking that the presence of an adult made her safe, Pamela climbed up off the ground. Wincing as she rubbed her grazed shin, she scowled across at the two Scales boys. "I reckon no one's safe wi' these two thugs on the loose. You should keep 'em chained up."

"Chained up, eh?" Mrs Scales scratched her head. "That's a very good idea, Pamela Groves.

Maybe you get fancy ideas like that from your dad."

Pamela shrugged. "He'd lock these two up if he knew 'ow they'd treated us."

"Aye, 'e used to be good at locking folk up." Mrs Scales turned to her sons. "How many times 'ave I collected your father from them police cells?"

"Too many times," Duncan griped. "An' always for nowt, too. I mean, what kind o' country locks people up for defendin' themselves?"

Vincent nodded enthusiastically. "Not Germany. If t' Germans win t' war, Dad'll be able to come 'ome. 'Ang on – didn't Albert say that two kids were snoopin' around after 'im t' other day?"

"Aye, 'e did," Duncan agreed. "He only got a good look at one of 'em. But I reckon it could 'ave been these two."

"We don't even know who Albert is," argued Tom.

"We've got better things to do than snoop after

your lodger," Pamela added.

Still watching from his hiding place, Sam knew that Pamela had said too much when he saw a mixture of surprise and triumph push Mrs Scales' caterpillar-thick eyebrows halfway up her wrinkled forehead.

The monstrous woman bent close to Pamela with a malicious grin. "An' how d'you know that 'e's my lodger?"

Pamela fired a worried glance towards Tom. "I... uh... we..."

Duncan grinned in triumph. "See, Ma! We told you these were t' snoopers."

"We'll know when Albert sees 'em!" Vincent said. "Where is 'e?"

"Out," Mrs Scales told them sharply. "He'll be back soon enough."

"What do we do wi' these two 'til then?" Duncan wondered.

"Let's give Pamela and 'er little friend a taste of 'er dad's medicine, shall we?" Sudden fury seemed to darken Mrs Scales' face as she pointed towards the nearest barn. "Take 'em in there and do as she suggested... tie 'em both up!"

"No! You can't!" Pamela howled as Vincent dragged her towards the building.

"You can't do that!" Tom seemed equally powerless to prevent Duncan from hauling him in the same direction. "It's illegal."

"So is ignoring *Keep Out* signs," cackled Mrs Scales, following them towards the barn doors.

*

Sam watched, aghast, as the two brothers dragged his friends into the barn. It was like watching a scene from the black-and-white Hollywood movies he'd watched with his mother in the theatres back home in Bethnal Green. That had been before the war broke out, when life had been normal – but there was nothing normal about this. Sam's mind whirred between the decoded message and the strange behaviour of the Scales family; something was very, very wrong. Part of him wished that this *was* a scene from one of those movies. At least then he'd have a script that told him what to do next, and there was usually a happy ending.

He was still trying to figure out his next move when a familiar figure crept from the shadows of one of the farm's outbuildings. Clearly preferring not to be seen, Lily checked left then right before dashing into the sanctuary of another patch of shade. She slowly navigated the terrace of buildings, skulking from one shadow to the next.

As she drew near to Sam's hiding place, he could see that distress and fear had creased her face into an anxious knot. Tears streamed down her wet cheeks as she sobbed silently.

Although desperate to tell his cousin that he was nearby, Sam managed to swallow his urge to call Lily's name. After all, if he was going to stand any chance of helping his friends, he would need to remain hidden – yet Lily needed his help, too, before she became the next hostage.

It was the group of starlings, which had returned

to the branches directly above Sam's head, that gave him the solution that he was looking for. As they flapped and hopped from branch to branch, squabbling like irritable toddlers, a storm of twigs and leaves and dislodged pine cones rained down on Sam's head.

Grabbing a handful of pine cones, he gently propelled them into the farm's courtyard. They hit the ground and bounced across the cobbles. Some pinged left; others ricocheted right. A couple, though, made it all the way to Lily's feet.

She wiped her cheeks clean as she turned to find out where they had come from. When she saw Sam, her green eyes were pulled wide by disbelief. Relieved to have hooked her attention, Sam stepped out from behind his tree and urged Lily to join him. He watched out for prying eyes or shrieks of alarm until his cousin reached the safety of the woodland. Hugging each other, they retreated out of sight into the scrum of tree trunks.

"They have Tom and Pamela," Lily sobbed. "They must have come looking for me but Duncan and

Vincent found them first."

"I know," Sam told her. "I sent them here."

"Why? What's wrong?"

Sam dragged the crumpled slip of paper from his pocket. "We went back to the beach, Lils. We saw someone sending more signals..."

"Signals?" Lily shook her head. "How? Was it Albert?"

"Morse code, Lils," Sam explained. "Soldiers use it to communicate. Naval ships, too. It can be sent by flashes of light."

"But I don't understand," Lily admitted. "Who would he signal to? The only things out in the ocean are fish."

He handed her the paper. "Read it."

Lily stared at the collection of roughly scribbled words. As she read the words aloud, her voice was barely above a whisper. "...diers arriving. Target school in forty eig..."

Sam waited, watching his cousin read, then reread, the words.

Finally, she shook her head. "It doesn't make any sense. What does it mean?"

"There are some letters missing. All we can do is fill in the gaps."

When Lily handed the paper back to Sam, it was as though the note were burning her fingers. "I don't understand, Sam. Who did he send this to?"

Sam shrugged. He had asked Tom and Pamela the same question, over and over again. They'd always arrived at the same terrifying answer. "The Germans?"

"Why?"

"They're targeting soldiers, Lils," Sam explained. "Look at the message. A new company moves into the school on Thursday – Corporal Timmins told me. That's forty-eight hours from last night, when he sent the message. I think the Germans are going to bomb the school and kill the soldiers. And someone's helping them!"

*

Having retreated even farther back into the woodland, the two children discussed their next move.

"We have to rescue Tom and Pamela," Sam insisted. "It's my fault that they're caught up in this. They're innocent."

"*We're* innocent," Lily reminded him. "It's Albert who is the guilty one, here."

Sam's mind was racing, consumed by the guilt of seeing his friends taken hostage. He'd sent them here. He was responsible. If Lily was right and it was Albert who had sent the messages, then all the trouble was under one roof, and they had to stop it.

"If we told Missus Scales..." Lily started.

"That won't work," replied Sam, his mind racing. "I'm pretty sure the Scales family are up to no good – they seem perfectly happy to be at war. It keeps them on top around here." Anger was turning his words to ash in his mouth and he found himself trembling. Sam shook himself. "We need to rescue Tom and Pamela first."

Lily shook her head. "They'll be safe – at least until Albert gets back. That gives us time to gather some evidence." Lily glanced back across at the stone farmhouse.

"How?"

"Albert has the attic room at the top of the house." Lily's finger jabbed towards a small window peering out from among the roof tiles.

"Where is he now?"

"Dunno. I saw him go out about an hour ago." Her nostrils flared. "He was smoking one of those disgusting cigarettes."

Sam thought hard. If there was any chance that Albert was up to no good, they had to do something about it, and fast. He nodded as a plan formed inside his head. "So, one of us needs to get inside his room."

Lily wrung her hands together. "We'll never get past Missus Scales. She's got a sixth sense for things that go on inside that house."

Sam scanned the farm buildings in search of inspiration. Finally, he clapped his hands together. "We need to get her out of the house."

"Oh, and how exactly are you going to do that?" Lily asked.

"I'm not," Sam said. "You are!"

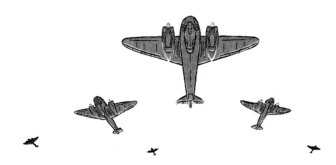

Chapter Seventeen
The Empty Bedroom

The plan was a simple one – and it worked perfectly.

From his hiding place at the corner of the stable block, Sam watched his cousin stroll into one of the smaller outbuildings. Moments later, she strolled out again, as though nothing had happened.

She wasn't alone. A dozen white and brown chickens hopped and flapped through the barn door behind her. They clucked excitedly, clearly happy to be out in the sunshine. None of them were meant to be there.

"Missus Scales! Help!" Lily cried, racing towards

the house. "The chickens have escaped."

In seconds, Duncan and Vincent's mother bolted into the yard.

"Useless girl!" she howled, swinging the head of her broom towards Lily. "How did you let this happen?"

Lily ducked away from the broom and didn't reply. She was too busy trying to swallow a fit of giggles as she watched her rotund host desperately trying to herd the chickens back towards the barn.

"Stupid birds!" Mrs Scales growled. "Get back in there, or one of you will be tonight's dinner."

With Mrs Scales fully occupied, Sam seized his opportunity, sprinting hard towards the house. He was up the two front steps and through the door in under ten seconds.

Lily quickly followed him into the hallway. "Go up three flights of stairs. Albert's room is the very last door."

Sam nodded and began to bolt up the bare, wooden stairs, two at a time.

"Be careful," Lily urged, "and be quick!"

*

As Lily returned to the yard under the pretence of helping Mrs Scales, Sam headed for the lodger's room. The stairs were steep but adrenaline rocketed Sam up all three flights in seconds. When he arrived at the narrow, wooden door, he was barely out of breath.

Still, he paused in front of the door for a second or two, collecting his thoughts. As exciting as this was, Sam also knew that it was important – potentially life-saving. After all, if he found evidence linking the Scales Farm lodger to the Germans, and maybe information about the school bombing itself, the authorities would have to listen to him. It was this sudden realisation that slowed him slightly, making him turn the door's iron handle with a little more caution.

The door was unlocked and swung open on squeaking hinges. Sam stepped into the room and instantly felt as though his hopes were leaking out through his feet.

At first glance, it looked as if no one lived there. The bed was made neatly, with sheets folded tightly at the corners. The writing desk had nothing on it. Even the chair in the corner of the room looked like it hadn't been sat on in weeks. In fact, the only obvious trace of Albert was the lingering smell of cigarette smoke and an ashtray half filled with crumpled butts, beneath a brass lamp on the bedside cabinet.

Although his whole body felt heavy with disappointment, Sam began to look for potential hiding places. He found nothing but clothes in the dresser drawers beneath the open window, and only shirts and trousers were hanging in the small wardrobe.

However, when Sam peered beneath the bed itself, he hit the jackpot. The suitcase felt heavy as he dragged it from its hiding place and his stomach churned like a whirlpool as he released both brass clasps and pulled open the case.

"No!" he hissed, as his eyes fell on more clothes

and shoes.

He pushed his fingers under Albert's belongings, hoping to find something important hidden beneath. But there was nothing in the case, nor in the room, which suggested that Albert was anything but a lodger.

Reluctantly, Sam admitted defeat. His initial buzz of excitement had now turned to a heavy churn of nausea. They had been wrong. Albert was nothing but a lodger and a well-respected member of the community who didn't like being followed, and Sam was a fool. He had put his friends in harm's way over nothing but his cousin's hunch.

Sam pushed the suitcase back under the bed and was about to stand up when his gaze fell upon something dark and thin that was tucked between the mattress and the bed frame. Immediately, his heart jumped back into his mouth.

It was easy to miss. In fact, if Sam hadn't been staring in disappointment at the space under the bed, he probably wouldn't have spotted it.

The small, leather ledger took a little work to wrestle free but when Sam managed to lift the mattress and tug it out, he found himself staring down at a book that had clearly been hidden on purpose. Its pages bulged with loose sheets and the warped covers were tied tightly together with a single length of twine. Sam took hold of one end, ready to pull it open.

"Who are you?"

Sam had been so preoccupied with removing the ledger that he had not heard the gentle *thud* of footsteps climbing the stairs, nor had he heard those same feet entering the bedroom.

Sam turned to face the newcomer.

A tall man with stern, angular features blocked the doorway. Accusing, dark eyes glared at Sam in recognition. "What are you doing in here?"

Sam didn't have a chance to reply. As soon as Albert saw what his intruder was looking at, he lunged towards him.

Sam rolled away but he wasn't fast enough – Albert crashed down on top of him. As a strong hand pinned Sam against the mattress, the lodger knocked the notebook onto the floor, where its pages spilled out. Smoke and ash poured from a cigarette which was still clamped between the lodger's fingers.

"You shouldn't be looking at that," Albert raged. "That's none of your business." Sam struggled to wriggle free but Albert was too powerful. Kicking and squirming didn't help, so Sam did the only thing that he could think of: he sank his teeth into the lodger's hand.

It was enough to weaken Albert's grip and, as a yelp from the lodger sent the smoking cigarette spinning onto the bedsheets, Sam rolled free and bolted for the bedroom door.

Half running and half falling, Sam raced back down the steps. Behind him, Albert's heavy footsteps gave chase, followed by the worrying smell of a smouldering blanket.

Sam burst from the house and out into the yard, closely followed by Albert. Both stopped momentarily in shock when they saw that the yard wasn't empty.

Two military jeeps were parked in front of the house and several soldiers stood talking to Lily, Tom and Pamela. Tom was rubbing his head and seemed subdued by shock; Pamela, on the other hand, seemed more than happy to tell two newly arrived soldiers exactly what had been going on as they began to interrogate Mrs Scales and her two sons as to why there were two children chained up in their barn.

Sam recognised one soldier as Corporal Timmins, who was lifting the stolen green bicycle into the back of a matching vehicle – but Sam no longer cared about remaining hidden.

"It's not just them," Sam shouted as he sped across the courtyard. "It's the lodger. He's a spy!"

All eyes turned to look at Sam and his chaser. Several soldiers turned and squared their shoulders in suspicion, responding to the strange situation.

Behind Sam, Albert suddenly abandoned his chase. Spooked by the presence of the soldiers, he veered right and bolted away from the group.

"Don't let him get away," Sam shouted, fixing Corporal Timmins with a desperate, pleading stare. "He's dangerous."

"Bring me that man," Corporal Timmins ordered, instructing his soldiers to give chase.

As two young soldiers sprinted across the courtyard, quickly gaining on the fleeing lodger, Mrs Scales saw her own opportunity to escape. After shoving an unsuspecting soldier to the ground, she shoulder-charged her way past another before disappearing into the gap between two of her outbuildings.

Her two sons weren't quite as quick or as lucky. As Vincent turned to make his own break for freedom, Pamela leapt onto his back, dragging him to the floor like a lioness felling a zebra. Duncan managed to evade the lunge of a soldier but not the outstretched foot of Tom, which sent the cumbersome teenager sprawling, face first, across the dusty cobbles.

Once both boys were bundled into the back of a military jeep, Corporal Timmins turned to Sam. "What exactly is going on here?" he asked.

"I told you," Sam panted. "They've been harbouring a spy."

The corporal seemed confused.

"It's the lodger," Lily told him. "We saw him signalling from the clifftop..."

"Signalling?" Corporal Timmins pressed both palms against his face, trying to massage away his perplexity. "How?"

"He was using horse code," Lily added.

"Morse code, Lils. It was Morse code," Sam corrected her. "They're targeting your soldiers."

"Sam decoded the message," Lily proudly announced. "Show him, Sam."

Corporal Timmins stared down at the scrap of paper that Sam handed to him. After a second or two, he looked back up at the two children and his expression was alarmingly serious. "Nobody will believe this. If you've made this up..."

Sam felt panic rising in his throat. "There's proof up there," he tried, pointed back towards the house. "I found a book of his, full of notes."

Shock sent the corporal's head rocking back and he turned to search for the lodger. "Do you have the book?"

Sam slapped his head and gazed up at the attic room. Thick, black smoke was now billowing through the open window. "I couldn't... I didn't... it's still in the room."

"It's evidence." Corporal Timmins looked anxiously towards the burning room. "If that goes up in smoke, it's just your word against his. And they'll –"

"– never believe a child." Sam felt a knot of failure twist his gut.

"Don't worry," Lily told them. "I'll get it!"

"NO!" Sam and the corporal howled together.

It was too late – Lily was already sprinting across the yard towards the house.

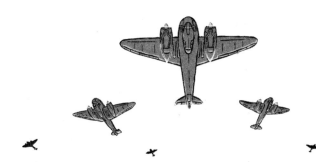

Chapter Eighteen
There's No Smoke without Fire

Although they were both only moments behind her, by the time Sam and Corporal Timmins raced through the farmhouse entrance, Lily had disappeared from view.

Already, thick arms of smoke were surging down the house's staircase, reaching for them like the swirling limbs of a kraken. Fingers of acrid mist reached down Sam's throat, pulling coughs and wheezes from his lungs. Beside him, the corporal's hacks and splutters confirmed that he was under a similar attack.

The soldier pulled his combat sweater over his mouth and nose in an attempt to repel the fire's offence. "Which way, Sam?"

They hadn't moved, yet already Sam was feeling disoriented. Above their heads, waves of thick black soot and smoke swirled and billowed like storm clouds. Through eyes that were already watering, Sam watched in horror as those swirls began to crawl down the walls and windows. They devoured everything, swallowing paintings, coat hooks and a hat rack, and even the day's sunlight.

"I can't see," Sam wheezed as the darkness began to cocoon him. He slashed his hands through the smoke, desperately trying to cut a pathway forward. "We need to find the stairs."

"Lily!" the soldier called. "Lily, come back, it's too dangerous."

When only silence responded, the soldier reached out to grab Sam and push him back to the door. "Get out, Sam. I'll find her."

Sam squirmed free of Corporal Timmins' grip, coughing up another lungful of soot and smoke. "No chance! The evidence is up there, and I know the way... if we don't get that, all this has been a waste of time."

"It's not worth dying for, Sam!"

"Maybe not," Sam said, beating the smoke back with his hands. "But Lily is. I'm not leaving without her."

Sam would never know whether it was simply coincidence or the result of his determined efforts that caused the plumes of smoke to retreat at exactly that moment. As though the fire itself were inhaling, the twisting billows shrank and briefly parted, giving Sam a glimpse through the hallway towards the staircase.

He threw himself forward, surging through the darkness like a desperate jungle explorer in search of lost treasure.

"This way," he told the corporal. "She'll be up here."

Together, they battled up the staircase. Daylight from second-storey windows lanced spears of brightness through the smoke, helping to light their way, but there was still no sight or sound of Lily. At the top of the first flight of stairs, Corporal Timmins dragged Sam to the floor.

"We have to keep beneath the smoke," he told him. Soot had already painted patches across his face like coal miners' finger marks. "There's still clean oxygen down here."

Sam couldn't help wondering if Lily had realised the same thing. He hoped so.

"How much farther?" the soldier asked.

"Another flight," Sam replied. Desperately trying to overcome his fears, he was preparing to resume his climb when from somewhere above them, a scream raced down the stairs.

"Lily!" gasped Sam. "She's hurt!"

Corporal Timmins placed a calming hand on Sam's shoulder. "At least she's alive."

"We need to find her." Both crawled up the stairs as fast as their suffering muscles could manage and, somehow, found themselves on the next landing. There, through the smoke, they were faced with more doors than they could possibly search in the time that was left before the fire devoured the whole house. Resolute, Sam began to crawl, but the soldier's grip on his arm was too strong.

"Wait! We need to know exactly where she is," he told Sam with a grave edge to his voice.

"LILY!" Sam yelled as panicked tears dried instantly on his face, leaving dry, salty streaks under his eyes. "Lils, we're coming. Where are you? We need to hear your voice!"

At first, there was no reply, not even a scream. In fact, as the smoke closed in on them again, Sam was beginning to fear the worst – until a weak but familiar sound reached out from close by.

"Was that an owl?" Corporal Timmins choked out, as a second, weak hoot followed the first.

Sam grinned as more tears were stolen from his cheeks, and then hooted back. "It's not an owl... that's Lily..." He was already crawling forwards, his resolve renewed.

They barely lifted their heads off the bare, wooden floor as they followed Lily's hoots. Sam could feel his chest tightening and his own hoots weakening. Lily's sounds were losing strength, too – they were all running out of time.

Sam and Corporal Timmins could no longer see the shapes made by the doorways and walls of the house. Using their fingers and palms to feel their way through the darkness, they frisked the walls and floor until they encountered a doorway.

The first room that they checked was empty, as was the second. By the time their hands told them that they had found a third room, Sam was fighting to stay awake. His chest burned as though fire was raging inside each lung and what air they did find to breathe seemed to burn his lips and tongue. Sam knew that this would be the last room that they checked.

"This way," Corporal Timmins urged. "She has to be in here!"

Sam's hoots sounded more like gargles, now, but he persisted anyway, fighting through the smoke in a desperate attempt to hear his cousin's reply.

Ash and fumes had replaced the oxygen and Sam could no longer battle the effects. His limbs felt heavier than lead and his head seemed welded to the floor. As his eyes closed, he gave one final gargle. Lily's own last hoot fell on deaf ears.

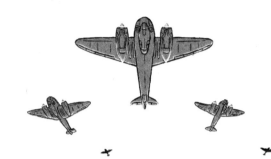

Chapter Nineteen
Bombs and Bandages

Hospitals can be very boring places. Aside from the hustle and panic of an emergency situation, things happen very slowly. Very quietly, too.

Sam had never been a patient in hospital before. He'd always imagined that those who did find themselves tucked beneath the starched, white sheets of a hospital bed would quickly be driven half mad by a cocktail of boredom and frustration.

Now, though, as a temporary resident of one of the hospital's embracing beds, he welcomed the peace and solitude. It gave his bruised body and strained mind the time and space to recover.

Sam barely remembered anything from the first twenty-four hours. They had passed him by in a blur of busy nurses, anxious doctors and what felt like an interrogation of worried eyes. He'd slipped in and out of sleep; whenever he had managed to drift off again, he'd been dragged awake by a searing pain in his throat and chest which made him wonder if he'd been eating glass and nails. He had heard the sound of voices by his bedside but his exhausted brain couldn't decipher their meaning, let alone form words of its own.

This time, though, it wasn't the pain in his throat or chest that dragged him from his drugged slumber – it was the rumbling *boom* of explosions. They were distant, but Sam would recognise that sound anywhere.

Sam's eyes snapped open as more explosions disturbed the hospital's tranquillity. Although the glow of the hospital lights made his eyes momentarily object, after a few anxious blinks, his gaze settled upon the concerned face of a young nurse. Her crisp, white apron looked as though it might have been made from one of the hospital's bedsheets.

"Good evenin', Samuel," she said politely. "How are you feeling?"

"Am I back in London?" Sam winced; every word hurt his damaged throat.

"Of course not," the nurse replied. "You're in Scarborough. Whatever makes you think you're in London?"

"Those explosions," Sam said. "It's exactly the same sound Jerry's bombs made back home."

The nurse fired a concerned glance over her shoulder as the windows rattled again.

"We'll be reet. Even Jerry isn't 'eartless enough to target hospitals. Though one of those air force soldiers told us they're aiming for t' primary school at Filey!"

"The school?" Sam gasped, and made himself cough. "They're dropping bombs on the school?"

The nurse nodded slowly. "An' from what we've 'eard, they 'aven't missed."

The news struck Sam like a blow. Tears of rage and frustration spilled onto his cheeks as the realisation struck that his and his friends' efforts had all been for nothing. They'd failed. The Germans had still managed to bomb the school.

*

Sam didn't remember falling asleep. Yet when he next opened his eyes, he realised that the sound of explosions had stopped. He could hear gentle movements around him as the nurses tiptoed between their patients. When he opened his eyes to bright daylight and glanced across at the large clock which perched above the ward's entrance doors, he saw that a whole night had passed since the bombing raid. Life in the hospital was returning to normal.

"Would you like something to eat?" one of the nurses asked him. Her tone was gentle and encouraging. "The energy will help your recovery."

Although his rumbling stomach answered the nurse's question for him, Sam's next thought had nothing to do with food.

"Where's Lily?"

The nurse responded with a puzzled expression. "Who?"

Sam ignored the sting in his chest as he shuffled into a seated position. "Lily. My cousin." His gaze scanned left and right, moving between the beds and patients that shared the ward. All seven beds were occupied. None of them contained Lily.

The nurse dropped her own gaze to a clipboard at the foot of Sam's bed. As she read from it, she said, "I'm sorry. There's no mention of anyone else."

Fear had wrapped its icy fingers around his heart. Its grip was tightening as he began to count the reasons why Lily might not be in the hospital with him. He could only think of one.

"Is she... dead?"

His question had transformed the nurse's pretty

face into an ugly scrunch of discomfort. As she backed away from his bed, Sam whispered his question again.

"Is Lily *dead*?"

The nurse was rescued by the loud slam of a door. The sound was quickly pursued by the clatter of hurried footsteps.

"Sam!" a familiar voice panted. "You're awake!"

"I should 'ope so!" a second voice added. "Lazy beggar's been sleepin' for t' best part o' two days."

Tom and Pamela hopped onto the foot of Sam's bed, perching together like a couple of cosy parrots. Their smiles and wide eyes told Sam that they were happy to see him.

Sam found it impossible to return their warmth. "She's dead, isn't she?"

"What?" The smile dropped from Tom's lips like melted ice.

Pamela leaned back as though she had just been slapped. "Who?"

"Lily," Sam said. "The nurse had no idea who she was. Is she dead?"

After a moment of frozen silence, both faces broke into grins.

"Dead?" Tom's face was contorted by mirth and sympathy. He nudged Pamela in the ribs. "I guess that's a ghost in the next room, then."

"Yup," Pamela giggled.

As a tsunami of relief hit him, Sam buried his head into his hands. He fought back tears as he said, "She's not dead?"

"Of course she's not dead," Tom replied. "She's next door, resting."

Pamela wagged a finger toward Sam. "Like you should be!"

Dragging the bedsheets away from his legs, Sam rolled to his left and dropped the soles of his bare feet onto the tiled floor. Cold gripped his skin. "Come on. Take me to her."

*

The neighbouring ward was a mirror image of the room that the trio had just left. Sam pushed through the double doors at such a pace that the hem of his hospital gown flapped like a sail. His feet beat out a round of applause as he rushed into the room.

A stern-looking matron looked up from her paperwork, glaring at the children over the top of her black spectacle frames. "Be quiet! This isn't a playground."

Ignoring her, Sam continued down the room. He checked the occupant of each bed. Part of him didn't believe what Tom and Pamela had told him. Part of him needed to see Lily for himself.

He found her sleeping in the fifth bay.

Tom joined Sam at the foot of Lily's bed. "What did I tell you?"

Pamela squeezed beside them. "She's looked better, but the doctors say she'll be sound."

Sam couldn't take his eyes from Lily. Her forehead was swathed in bandages, hiding burns that her hospital notes classified as superficial. More bandages protected scorched fingertips that would probably remain sore for several weeks.

"I did this," Sam muttered. "This is my fault."

"What are you talking about?" Tom asked.

"I should have gone into the house first," Sam replied. "Then, none of this would have happened."

"Rubbish!" Pamela insisted. "You're t' reason she's still alive. It was you who found her."

Sam was preparing to argue when his attention was stolen by the sharp rap of military-grade heels against floor tiles.

"Glad to see you up and about, Sam!"

When Sam turned, he found himself staring

up at the reassuring face of Corporal Timmins. Unlike Sam and Lily, the soldier looked relatively unscathed.

"It's more than I can say for Lily," Sam told him. "She's never going to forgive me, is she?"

Corporal Timmins studied Tom's and Pamela's faces, looking for answers.

"He thinks it's his fault that she got hurt," Tom explained.

"Reckons he should 'ave been t' hero," Pamela added. "Obviously thinks us females aren't capable o' thinkin' or actin' for ourselves."

Suddenly understanding, Corporal Timmins smiled at Sam warmly, gently rubbing the boy's head before easing himself into a spare chair.

"She looks a little better," whispered the corporal.

Pamela nodded. "The doctors reckon she's makin' good progress."

Smiling, the corporal looked across at Sam

and said, "That's good. It means she's over the worst." When Sam didn't respond, the man continued. "I've asked the nurses to put you in the bed beside Lily," he said, gesturing to an empty bed behind him. Almost as though she had been waiting for her cue, the nurse who had been tending to Sam bustled in from the end of the ward at that moment, carrying a small pile of Sam's clothes and belongings.

The soldier paused as the woman prepared Sam's bed, and then jerked as though he had just remembered something important. "I almost forgot – the base commander wants to meet you both. I told him I'd ask you if it was OK."

"Why would the base commander want to meet me?" came a small croak from the hospital bed.

The weak voice shocked them all, whipping their heads around as if they were each attached to chains.

"Lily!" Sam gasped, leaping out of his chair. "You're awake."

His young cousin squirmed painfully in her

hospital bed, struggling to prop herself up. "How can I sleep with you lot nattering away like washer-women?"

Grinning, Tom said, "She's definitely feeling better."

Lily turned to gaze at her cousin. "I'm sorry, Sam."

"*You're* sorry?"

Lily nodded. "You told me not to go into the house. I should have listened."

Sam shook his head. "I should have stopped you."

"He's only jealous," Pamela leaned towards Lily and winked. "I think 'e wanted all t' glory for 'imself."

Lily laughed, then raised a hand to her throat and winced. "There's nothing heroic about getting burned."

Suddenly, her eyes widened as she threw a

bandaged hand to cover her mouth. "The book! Oh no... the school! Sam, what day is it?"

Sam couldn't answer.

"It's Friday," offered Pamela. "Tell 'em about the school," she urged Corporal Timmins.

Sam reached for one of Lily's wrapped hands, holding it gently. He knew what was coming.

The soldier sighed. "It took a direct hit last night. The main building was completely destroyed."

There was a short silence. Tears rolled down Lily's cheeks as she raised her bandaged hands. "So, all this was for nothing?"

"Not quite," Corporal Timmins shook his head. "Thanks to your hard work finding and decoding the message, we had a head start on the bombers. You bought us some valuable time."

The corners of his mouth twitched towards a smile as he continued. "We couldn't stop the bombing raid, but we did have time to evacuate the school. Thanks to you lot, we were able to save over two hundred men."

Sam and Lily swapped satisfied smiles.

"So Albert *was* spying! I knew it." Lily cried hoarsely. "I always knew there was something –"

Corporal Timmins silenced Lily with a gentle wave of his hand. "That's why I'm here as well, Lily. I have some news about that, too. When I found you, you were already unconscious. Albert's cigarette must have set his blanket on fire and it went up like summer hay in a lightning storm. I've never seen a blaze like it." He paused, perhaps searching for the right words. "Let's just say, much longer and we wouldn't be talking like this."

Lily glanced at Sam, whose nod confirmed that the corporal's story was true. "It was Corporal Timmins who rescued you," Sam told her.

"It was a joint effort, Lily," the soldier added. "Sam was very brave..."

Sam fixed his gaze on the hospital's tiled floor. He didn't feel very brave.

"...and when I got to you, there was something in your hand."

Sam looked up. Lily's eyes were filled with hope. "The book?"

"Yes. A few of the pages were singed but it was all in one piece." Corporal Timmins paused.

Sam couldn't wait any longer. "And? What did it have inside?" he pressed the soldier.

The corporal's heavy gaze swept from child to child, then he took a breath. "It was a book... of poetry."

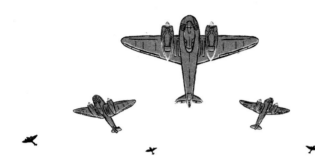

Chapter Twenty
Telegrams and Train Trips

All four children's mouths dropped open simultaneously.

"Poetry?" Sam repeated, incredulous. "What do you mean?"

"Albert, the lodger at Scales Farm," Corporal Timmins explained gently, "was a soldier who went away to fight when war broke out. When he came home with an injury, he was very traumatised by his experience. He also came home to find that his young family —" The corporal paused to find the right words. "That his family and his home had succumbed to a bombing raid. That is why he stays with Mrs Scales and her family."

Sam's mind seemed to have jammed like a cog with broken teeth. He sank onto his own bed and stared, frozen, at Corporal Timmins as this new information trickled through him. He was speechless.

Lily, however, wasn't. "No," she said defiantly. "He could still be a spy. We found his cigarettes on the clifftop," she announced, as though that settled the matter.

"Yes." Corporal Timmins nodded, speaking in the same delicate tone. "Albert's doctor has advised him to spend time outdoors. He has moved to Filey for the sea air and spends a lot of time writing poetry by the water to help him deal with his feelings." The soldier sighed heavily. "The effect that the war has had on that young man... it's impossible for any of us to understand."

"He avoids people..." Sam muttered, beginning to piece together Albert's strange behaviour.

The corporal nodded again. "Loud noises, busy places, even young children" – he glanced at Lily – "tend to bring back terrible memories for the poor man."

Lily looked confused. "Why did he run, then?" she asked.

"The mind of a soldier who has experienced the horrors of war is easily spooked," Corporal Timmins explained. "He was simply frightened."

The children were silent. Sam's insides twisted horribly as he thought back to the day when he had followed the paranoid ex-soldier through town. It was no wonder the man had become agitated.

Finally, Tom spoke. "What about Missus Scales? Vincent and Duncan?"

"We found evidence under the house of a stone cellar full of black-market food – that usually means hard labour or a fine, at the very least."

"An' they tied us up!" Pamela interrupted, indignantly. "An' one o' them boys gave our Sam a black eye."

"Which was very wrong," added the corporal.

"We'll make sure that they are punished. In the meantime," he said with a deep breath, "there's still a spy somewhere in Filey. That's our biggest concern, now."

"Do you know who it could be?" asked Pamela eagerly.

"Not yet," said the corporal grimly, "but we're just becoming aware now of the scale of the problem. We think that whoever it is has been passing messages all over the country for months. It would help to explain a few other odd things that have happened recently."

The children began to talk quickly among themselves. They had been completely wrong about Albert but it still left them with so many unanswered questions.

Sam remembered the other item that they had found up on Filey Brigg: the large, gold ring. A new wave of regret washed over him as he recalled how they had taken it, convinced that it was another sign of Albert's guilt.

The children's discussion was halted as two

nurses came to tend to Lily. They had barely finished changing the dressings on her hands when the clatter of more footsteps rang out from the hospital corridor.

"Sounds like someone's in a right 'urry," complained the oldest nurse. "I've 'eard marchin' bands make less racket!"

The noise grew louder as the footsteps switched from a walk to a run. Moments later, the doors to the ward crashed open, slamming against the walls and drawing startled yelps from several patients. Yet that noise was nothing compared to the cries and wails that followed as two red-headed women thundered towards Lily's bed.

Shock forced Sam onto his feet before two arms that he had missed more than he'd realised wrapped around him in a hug which threatened him with suffocation. He saw Lily disappear into a similar embrace.

"Mum?" he finally gasped.

He squirmed as his cheeks were assaulted by dozens of soft kisses, and then winced as Joan

Hunt gave her son a swift clip to the ear.

"What were you *thinking*?!" she shrieked as she pulled him towards her again and squeezed him tightly. He felt his face grow damp as his mother's kisses were joined by a stream of warm tears. Gently, he eased himself free and gazed down into eyes which blazed with love.

"It's OK, Mum," he assured her. "We're fine."

"*Fine*?!" Aunt Peg howled, clasping a hand to each of her daughter's cheeks as she stared at her. "You call *this* 'fine'? All those nights we dragged you to the shelter, and as soon as we send you away to where you're safe, you rush into the first burning building you see!"

"I'll be OK, Mum," Lily said. "It's not as bad as it looks."

"Let me speak to the doctors about that," Aunt Peg insisted, before throwing her arms around her little girl again.

Sam couldn't shake off his confusion as he sat back down. "But Mum, what are you doing here?"

"Corporal Timmins here sent us a telegram yesterday," she explained. "He told us all about what you two have been up to."

Aunt Peg looked across at Sam. "Scared us half to death, he did. I was sure it was bad news. *Never* do that again, do you hear?"

Sam shuddered at the thought of his mother receiving a telegram. Since the troops had been deployed, a telegram at the door had only meant one thing: the death of a loved one. Now, he understood the two women's joy at finding their children alive and well.

"We got the first train from London," his mother explained. "Soldiers were waiting for us at the station – they brought us straight here."

"But... why... how?" Sam's head was spinning with a scramble of thoughts and emotions. "Where will you stay?"

"They can stay with us, Sam."

It was then that Sam noticed that a third woman had joined them at Lily's bedside. Mrs Ward looked pale and tired, and Sam again felt a pang of guilt as he thought about how worried she must have been.

Sam was just about to apologise when Corporal Timmins stepped forwards. "Right. Well, I'm going to head off, now. Pam, Tom, do you two want a lift back to Filey?"

The two children nodded and rose out of their chairs. Each one said goodbye to Sam and Lily, then followed the corporal from the ward.

Just as the door swung shut behind the soldier, Sam's eyes fell upon the pile of objects that the nurse had brought through from the next room. Albert's gold ring was tucked neatly between the folded and laundered clothes, and Sam suddenly felt very strongly that he didn't want to keep it any longer. It needed to be returned to its owner.

"Corporal Timmins! Wait!" he shouted, drawing appalled looks from the patients and nurses around the ward. Slightly abashed and ignoring the searing pain in his throat, he gabbled, "Missus Ward, please could you catch Corporal Timmins and give this to him?" He held out the large ring to his host, feeling the shame of his mistake burning his fingers. "We found it on the Brigg. Tom and Pam can explain –"

"Missus Ward? Are you all right?"

Sam's mother had gripped Mrs Ward under the elbow to stop her from hitting the ground, as her knees seemed to have buckled underneath her at the sight of the ring. Sam sat, flabbergasted, as Joan Hunt steered the young woman onto the end of Sam's bed, where she sat, trembling, and held out her hands to take the ring from Sam. She was breathing hard, her face as white as the hospital sheets.

At the end of the ward, the doors were swinging again and Corporal Timmins poked his head back through the opening, looking puzzled. Sam caught a glimpse of Pam and Tom waiting in the corridor as the doors closed and the soldier walked carefully back across the tiles towards where Aunt Peg and Joan were looking apprehensively at Mrs Ward.

"Missus Ward?" Sam asked tentatively.

She was still perched on his crisp, white bedsheets, rocking herself gently back and forth. The large, man's ring was now hidden from view, clutched tightly in the woman's fists as she cradled it in her lap. Her eyes were closed and she was taking deep, steadying breaths.

"Is everything all right?" asked Corporal Timmins, sounding concerned, as he rounded the end of the bed and looked into Mrs Ward's face.

Sam quickly explained about the man's ring that they had found, which he had supposed must belong to Albert, but trailed off as Mrs Ward opened her eyes, which looked bloodshot and watery. She stared up at the adults standing around the bed and suddenly, she looked frightened.

Sam's gaze slipped from Mrs Ward's face to his mother, whose hand was still resting on the young woman's shoulder. Joan Hunt's own wedding ring looked worn and scratched, but Sam knew how much she treasured it.

All at once, images poured into Sam's mind as though he were watching a film reel. He saw Mr Ward's slippers in the sitting room and the too-big bicycle that Sam himself had ridden just days before. Then, he imagined that he could see Mrs Ward walking up on Filey Brigg, wearing her husband's wedding ring on the golden chain around her neck like a priceless talisman – except that she wasn't walking, now... she was lying on her front, propped up on her elbows in the grass and flashing a large torch out to sea.

Could it be?

A tidal wave of realisation crashed over Sam. The film inside his head was speeding up and his thoughts were coming so fast that he felt dizzy. Mrs Ward had moved into the area alone but no one had ever met her husband; she had taken up a job at the post office; she ran unknown errands in the evenings; she had even washed Sam's white stones clean of the message he had intercepted – *her* message! Sam felt as though the heavy stones had plunged into his stomach when he remembered that he himself had told Mrs Ward about the hundreds of soldiers that would be moving into the local school.

Stunned, Sam looked at Mrs Ward, his kind, warm, loving host. Her eyes were fixed on the tiled hospital floor and Sam could tell that she was thinking hard. "Missus Ward..." he started, hardly able to believe what he was thinking, "did you drop this ring up on Filey Brigg?"

The woman's eyes widened momentarily and then tears spilled down her cheeks as she ran her narrow fingers over the object in her hand. When she spoke, Sam noticed a change in the way she pronounced her husband's name.

"It belonged... to my Helnrich."

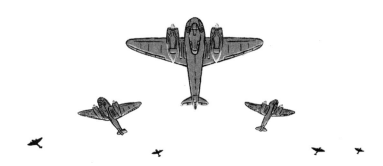

Chapter Twenty-One
Tyres as Thick as Liquorice

Three weeks passed before Sam's mother returned to London with Aunt Peg. By then, Lily had already been out of the hospital for a while and her scars were well on the way to healing. Life felt as though it was returning to normal – well, as normal as life can be during wartime.

Mrs Ward had been taken away the very same day that Sam had returned her husband's wedding ring to her. Sam had not seen anything that had followed first hand, but word had quickly spread through the village and Pamela and Tom had wasted no time in bringing every scrap of news they could find back to the hospital.

The first thing that Sam heard was that Corporal Timmins and his men had searched Mrs Ward's house. There, they had found that the garden shed – the only part of the property which Sam had never entered – was filled with maps, messages and information that Mrs Ward had been receiving through the post office from agents all over the country and as far away as America, and forwarding on to an address in Europe.

Following that, information came in small bursts here and there, and it was hard to know what was gossip and what was true. Generally, however, it seemed to be a known fact that Mrs Ward had actually been born in Scotland. She had married a German man named Heinrich at a young age and had lived in Germany for many years. When Heinrich had been killed in conflict at the start of the war, Mrs Ward had lost everything, and had agreed to work for the German military. She had moved to Filey, concocting a story about her husband's badly timed conscription, and had set up her 'post box' operation.

Sometimes, Sam caught himself forgetting that

Mrs Ward wasn't who she had said she was. He felt ashamed on several occasions when he found himself missing her clifftop garden, her excellent cooking and the loving way in which she used to say his name.

It didn't feel real, somehow. She had welcomed him into her home and he still believed that she was a caring, intelligent and kind woman. He couldn't quite bring himself to be angry with her just for wanting to take up her husband's fight on her side of the war. He spent long hours stewing over the mistake he had made in thinking that he knew how a spy should look and act. Now, he was just beginning to realise that there were many sides to every story – even war.

Since the fire at Scales Farm, Sam had been fighting a daily battle with guilt. While Corporal Timmins had told him countless times that the fire had been an accident, Sam felt terrible about the damage that had been done to the farmhouse in Muston. He had enquired after Albert but all the corporal had said was that Albert had found new lodgings and that there were no hard feelings. He also knew that the Scales family were still under investigation, but found that he didn't worry about their misfortunes quite as much.

Although Lily's burns had healed and the doctors had promised that her scars would vanish entirely within the year, Sam knew that his cousin had scars that no one could see. For the first few weeks after the fire, he could hear her crying out in her sleep and only when her nightmares had receded had Aunt Peg allowed herself to leave for London.

Sam and Lily had been taken in by Mr and Mrs Hargraves, who owned the grocery store. Having heard about their exploits and promising to look after the two children as if they were her own, Mrs Hargraves pulled out all the stops to keep her word. She was a pleasant woman who treated Lily like a daughter, and it wasn't long before the two were inseparable.

Sam loved seeing Lily getting on so well with their new host. After the miserable time that his cousin had endured at Scales Farm, Sam was happy that Lily was finally beginning to enjoy living in Yorkshire. However, there were times when he felt a little left out and so he was glad when Mr Hargraves approached him outside the shop one day with a proposition.

"I 'ope you two scruffy oiks aren't goin' to stand there all day – you'll be scarin' off me customers."

Sam and Tom were standing on the pavement outside the shop's window. An icy chill had been blowing in from the North Sea for the past few days but today, it was biting at their skin particularly hard. Sam had to concentrate to stop his teeth from chattering.

The shopkeeper jabbed his thumb towards a small rectangle of card wedged into the inside frame of the grocery store's window. "Now that you're all healed up, how d'you fancy a job for t' winter?" He grinned at Sam, then retreated into the warmth of the shop, leaving the boys alone again.

Sam's eyes settled on the notice and Tom read it aloud. "Grocery boys wanted. Pay bad. Bicycle old. Work hard. Boss grumpy. Enquire within."

Everything about the handwritten advert should have sent Sam running a mile. After all, bad pay and hard work is never a great combination – his dad had always told him as much – but, as much as Sam was enjoying Filey's quiet life and the little town's tranquil charm, he was getting a little bored. He was missing the hustle and bustle of London's crowded streets. Sharing his home city with hundreds of thousands of other people had its drawbacks, but there was also an excitement and a buzz that came from such incredible variety. Although he didn't miss Hitler's bombs, he did sometimes yearn to be back in London.

"It'd give me something to do," Sam mused. "Besides, it's the least I can do when Mister Hargraves is letting me and Lily stay here." He knew that the last delivery boy had been dismissed not long after the Scales' cellar had been raided, but hadn't thought it polite to ask his new host any more questions on the matter.

"There's plenty to do already," Tom reminded him. "We've still got miles of beaches to explore and there are loads of cliffs to climb. Hey, I forgot to tell you – Trudy Jones found a massive fossil in the caves at Flamborough yesterday."

Sam gave his shoulders a weak shrug. "We won't be able to do any of those things when the weather turns. Pamela says that the beach is no place to be when there's a gale blowing in. Filey's a summer town."

Tom gazed at the advert, shaking his head. "If you ask me, it sounds like it should come with a government warning. You won't catch me applying for that."

Sam stepped forwards, ignoring him. The familiar shop bell jangled somewhere above their heads as Tom followed Sam into the warm shop. Mr Hargraves beamed at the pair of them.

"Just wait 'til I tell t' wife. She said me ad would scare folk off – and now, here are two strappin' lads!"

Before Tom had a chance to explain that he wasn't there to apply, Mr Hargraves ushered them past his serving counter and into the shop's storeroom.

"Just watch you don't bump yourselves on those boxes," he warned, guiding them between two stacks of wooden containers marked *flour*. "We've 'ad new stock sent through and I'm still in t' process of unpackin' it all."

"What does the job involve?" Sam asked.

"Well, like me card says, it's rubbish pay, hard work, and I'm grumpy. That's about it, really."

"How much?" Tom asked.

Mr Hargraves scratched his head for a second, then said, "Well, if you asked me wife, she'd tell you that I'm *very* grumpy."

"No, no, no," Tom sniggered. "I meant, how much is the pay?"

"Oh! To be honest, it's mostly weekend work and I can't give you much more than a shillin' or two," the shopkeeper admitted. "But you'll get lots more in tips."

"Tips?" Sam asked.

"Aye," Mr Hargraves nodded. "Most o' me customers are older folk and not all of 'em have any grandchildren."

"What's that got to do with tips?" Tom asked.

The grocer continued, "Those folk wi' no grandkids still get their full rations. Eggs, flour, milk, meat and sweets."

He winked at them before explaining, "Those coupons can be used in me shop, so what tends to 'appen is they give me delivery lads their weekly ration of sweets as a tip. Me last lad," the grocer added with a slightly stiffened expression, "used to get over ten rations each week."

As Sam and Tom tried to calculate how many sweets that would add up to, Mr Hargraves helped them out. "Basically, you can 'ave as many sweets as you like."

"We could sell them at school," Tom whispered to Sam. "Pamela knows loads of kids."

Sam turned to his friend. "We?"

Ignoring Sam's question, Tom continued to quiz the grocer. "Your ad mentions a bicycle. How old is it?"

Mr Hargraves tried his best to hide a guilty expression behind the hand that massaged his chin. "Hmm, I knew you'd ask me about t' bicycle. Now, bear wi' me for a moment, 'cause I've got a bit of a confession to make." The grocer disappeared through another door, leaving the two friends alone in his store room.

Tom fired a knowing sneer in Sam's direction. "Told you, didn't I? It's probably some kind of rusty death trap."

Sam was still puzzled by his friend's earlier choice of words. "You said '*we*'. I thought you were against this job."

"I am," Tom waved his friend's question away. "But I'll still help you sell the sweets. We can split the profits, fifty-fifty."

"Fifty-fifty?" Sam spluttered. "Are you having a laugh?"

Before Tom could reply, Mr Hargraves returned to the store room. When Sam and Tom saw what he'd brought with him, their jaws fell open like a couple of old coat pockets.

"I'm sorry, I should've amended me advert," Mr Hargraves admitted. "I've recently upgraded me company transportation."

Sam and Tom both stared at the two gleaming, red Raleigh bicycles that Mr Hargraves had just rolled into the room. The wheels and handlebars shone silver and the tyres were so new and fat that they resembled thick rolls of liquorice.

"I 'ad these delivered t' other day," the grocer continued. "They might be a bit on t' big side, but I've 'ad baskets fitted to t' front and I can 'ave the seats and 'andlebars adjusted for you."

The boys stood looking at the bicycles, their eyes blazing with the lust and hunger of a lion eyeing fresh meat.

Smiling broadly, the shopkeeper wheeled the brand new bicycles towards the two boys. "So, 'ave I got myself two new delivery lads?"

241

Sam's reply was the kind of smile that his lips hadn't given for as long as he could remember. As his fingers embraced the unblemished handlebars of his brand new bicycle, he decided that life as an evacuee definitely had its perks.

THE END.

How much can you remember about the story? Take this quiz to find out!

1. What is the name of the town Sam is evacuated to?

2. What building is targeted by bombs after being used to house soldiers?

3. What is 'Code-Cracking for Beginners' in the story?

4. How did Corporal Timmins send a message to Sam's mum?

Answers: 1. Filey 2. (St. Margaret's) Primary School 3. a library book 4. a telegram

Challenge

Can you write a secret message in Morse code? You could write it with dots and dashes, or use a buzzer or a light.

Can you crack the code below?

A	· —	J	· — — —	S	· · ·
B	— · · ·	K	— · —	T	—
C	— · — ·	L	· — · ·	U	· · —
D	— · ·	M	— —	V	· · · —
E	·	N	— ·	W	· — —
F	· · — ·	O	— — —	X	— · · —
G	— — ·	P	· — — ·	Y	— · — —
H	· · · ·	Q	— — · —	Z	— — · ·
I	· ·	R	· — ·		

··—·/··/···/····/ ·—/—·/—··/
—·—·/····/··/·——·/···/

Discussion Time

? How many items can you remember from Sam's evacuee rucksack?

? How has the author used the dialogue to create characters who speak differently from one another?

? Do you think evacuating Sam and Lily to Yorkshire was a good idea? Why or why not?

? How do you feel toward the character of Mrs Ward?

Discover more from Twinkl Originals...
Continue the learning! Explore the library of Code-Cracking for Beginners activities, games and classroom resources at twinkl.com/originals.

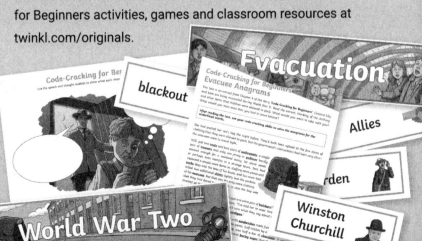

Welcome to the world of Twinkl Originals!

Board books for ages 0-3

Picture books for ages 3-7

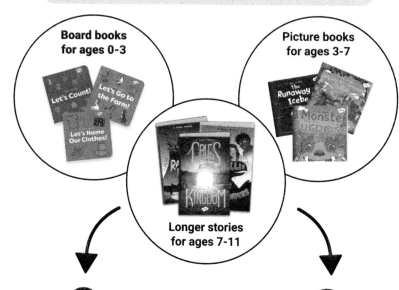

Longer stories for ages 7-11

Books delivered to your door

Enjoy original works of fiction in beautiful printed form, delivered to you each half term and yours to keep!

1   Join the club at twinkl.com/book-club.

2   Sign up to our Ultimate membership.

3   Make your selection – we'll take care of the rest!

The Twinkl Originals app

Now, you can read Twinkl Originals stories on the move! Enjoy a broad library of Twinkl Originals eBooks, fully accessible offline.

Search 'Twinkl Originals' in the App Store or on Google Play.

LOOK OUT FOR THE NEXT BOOK CLUB DELIVERY

It is 1916. A spindly tree stands in No Man's Land during the First World War amid wooden stumps and razor-sharp wire.

Hatched into the horrors of war, two birds sit in the tree. Humans live in trenches on either side – but are they friends or enemies? Can the birds' plan to sing for peace finally see an end to the years of danger?

COMING OCTOBER 2021

Look out for the digital eBook release at twinkl.com/originals